ISBN 978-1-331-62394-6
PIBN 10214448

English
Français
Deutsche
Italiano
Español
Português

www.forgottenbooks.com

Mythology Photography **Fiction**
Fishing Christianity **Art** Cooking
Essays Buddhism Freemasonry
Medicine **Biology** Music **Ancient
Egypt** Evolution Carpentry Physics
Dance Geology **Mathematics** Fitness
Shakespeare **Folklore** Yoga Marketing
Confidence Immortality Biographies
Poetry **Psychology** Witchcraft
Electronics Chemistry History **Law**
Accounting **Philosophy** Anthropology
Alchemy Drama Quantum Mechanics
Atheism Sexual Health **Ancient History**
Entrepreneurship Languages Sport
Paleontology Needlework Islam
Metaphysics Investment Archaeology
Parenting Statistics Criminology
Motivational

THE BAITED TRAP. Page 9.

MODEL LANDLORD.

BY

MRS. M. A. HOLT,

AUTHOR OF "JOHN BENTLEY'S MISTAKE," AND "WORK AND REWARD."

————

NEW YORK
National Temperance Society and Publication House,
No. 58 READE STREET.
——
1876.

ORPHANS' STEREOTYPE FOUNDRY, CHURCH CHARITY FOUNDATION, BR'KLYN.

CONTENTS.

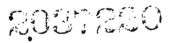

4 *Contents.*

THE MODEL LANDLORD

CHAPTER I.

THE GILDED MAN-TRAP.

"HOW strangely you talk, Weston; you do not seem willing to admit that the man possesses a single good quality. Why, sir, I believe that Andrew Freeland, to-day, is as good as half of your 'church men' who profess to be so much better than anybody else."

"There are undoubtedly worse men in our community than Andrew Freeland," was the low answer.

"And but few better ones," was the quick reply. "I tell you again, that there are scores of men in our village that we could better spare from our midst than Andrew Freeland.   A more generous, whole-souled man, you cannot find in the entire community, even if you look over your long roll of church members."

"I do not quite agree with you in regard to Freeland, Mr. Payne. I think that we have many better men than he, and I know of but few that I regard a greater curse to our beautiful village than this same man that you seem to regard so highly.   He may be a generous man in some respects, yet I think the word illy applies to one who takes the husband's and father's money in exchange for strong drink.   I tell you, Payne, I do not have much confidence in the moral principles of a rum-seller."

"There it is again.   Weston, you are growing crazy, I really believe. Freeland a rum-seller, because he owns a first-class hotel, and conducts his business in a quiet, orderly manner! You might well apply the word 'rumseller' to either Butler or Peck, but it is a perfect shame to call Andrew Freeland such a name." ·

"But he is one, just as much as either Butler or Peck. They have only taken a step or two farther in the business, and if the word rumseller applies to them, it does to him also."

"And so you would class Andrew Free-land with such men as keep our low, dirty saloons, and place him upon the level with creatures that are only half human;" and an angry flush rested for a moment upon the speaker's face:

"I doubt if any man is half human that

deals out alcohol as a beverage to his brother. I tell you, it is pretty wicked business,
let it be conducted in any way. There may
be different grades in the profession, but I
cannot see that any one presents a better
moral aspect than the others. Freeland begins the work of making drunkards and Butler and Peck finish the job. Each of these
men is well qualified to work in his station,
and all are doing the devil's business in a way
peculiarly their own. Their master is undoubtedly satisfied with the work of each, for
they are true to his interests."

"And so you will not admit that Freeland
is any better than these despicable men that
have been named. While he is engaged in
nothing but strictly lawful business, and
dealing fairly and honestly with all, they
allow the worst forms of vice to be enacted

in their underground dens. While he uses judgment and discretion in selling liquor, they deal it out readily to all, and even seek to lure our young boys into the baited traps."

"If this is true of them," said Mr. Weston, interrupting the speaker, "they infringe upon the rights of Freeland. It is his business to entrap the young and unsuspecting."

"I do not believe that Andrew Freeland ever by word or look sought to lead a boy or young man into the habit of drinking liquor ;" and Mr. Payne spoke in a very decided way.

"He has by deed, however, for he has fitted up a very elegant saloon, and adorned it in a way that will attract innocent eyes. He does not need to speak or even look, to get his victims in. They will go themselves, while you could not urge them to even step into such places as are kept by Butler and Peck. They cannot detect the enemy in the fine surroundings of Mr. Freeland, while they can readily discover him, peering from every corner of the blackened walls where the finishing work is done. I do not think that Butler and Peck can accomplish much, when they seek to lead the young and innocent into their dens. I really believe that Freeland is the most dangerous man that we have in town. His fine hotel, that he conducts so orderly, is nothing but a man-trap to catch human souls, while these other dens are the places where their victims are entirely crushed, and tortured to death. When a human being once gets upon the "enchanted ground," it does not require much effort to keep him there until utterly ruined. The greatest trouble is, to persuade him to cross the border lines, and this work Andrew Freeland is doing finely."

"I am glad that I do not see through your eyes, Henry Weston, or possess such fanatical notions. I regard Andrew Freeland as a true manly fellow, one that would not intentionally harm a single human being. Next week I am intending to remove to this same 'man-trap,' as you term it, which will be my home for awhile at least."

"Will Philip go also?" was the inquiry.

"To be sure, Mr. Weston. Do you suppose that I shall allow my son to be homeless while I have plenty of money, and good 'quarters' for myself? No, I shall have the management of my boy myself, and not leave him to the tender mercy of friends and relatives."

"I should much rather he would live with

entire strangers, than to spend his early
years in the fine gilded hotel of Andrew
Freeland, if he were my son. I tell you, Payne,
little Phil is too young and innocent to learn
the lessons that he will receive there in the
next two years;" and saying this Mr. Weston
rose to go.

"I do not think that my boy will be injured by boarding and lodging in the hotel
of Andrew Freeland, for two years or even
five. Any way, I shall borrow no trouble
upon his account just now. Andrew Freeland is not so bad a man, after all that you
have said about him. I will not stay to hear
him abused any longer," and Payne also arose
to go.

"You will yet understand the man better,
but it may be too late," Weston said, as he
walked away toward the pleasant farm-house

which he called his own just out of the busy town.

These two men had been sitting upon the stone steps of one of the large mercantile establishments of A——, within sight of the showy hotel of Mr. Freeland. The landlord had been making extensive repairs upon the building which he occupied, and this was the way that Mr. Weston and Payne became engaged in the conversation just recorded. Mr. Weston was an earnest advocate of temperance, and did not hesitate to speak out his honest convictions in regard to it, wherever he chanced to be. All kinds of abusive names had been applied to him, but the "one idea man," "crazy reformer" and "temperance fanatic" kept straight along in the path which he had chosen, turning neither to the right nor left. It was true, that his ideas in regard to temperance were somewhat in advance of slow moving public opinion, yet as he was a man of wealth and influence in the community, people were not wholly indifferent to the principles which he advocated. And George Payne was also a man of wealth and position, living an easy, aimless life, drifting about just where the winds and tide of worldliness carried him. Yet he was regarded by those who knew him as a man of moral worth and principle; and if these elements of human greatness can dwell in a soul drifting aimlessly upon the ocean of existence, George Payne really possessed them. Even Henry Weston, who understood the man perfectly, said, "He is a good fellow, but sadly blinded by the false teachings of the world."

Only a few months before, good Mrs.

Payne had died, and left her husband and child alone in the world. With her death, the light and happiness went out in the old home, and George Payne became sad and restless. He could not remain in the place where so many happy hours had been passed, and so he went away for a few weeks, leaving little Phil in the care of his sister, a kind Christian lady who would gladly have kept the bright active boy until he should become a man. But Mr. Payne returned suddenly, saying that it was impossible for him to remain away from his only idol, little Phil, and so he took the boy and went back into the old home. Yet the old spirit of unrest and disquietude followed him, and soon he decided to leave the place haunted by so many dear remembrances, and take up his abode in the large stylish hotel, kept by Mr. Freeland. Perhaps he came to such a conclusion, knowing if he remained there, amidst the active bustle and gayety of hotel life, he would in some measure forget the past, and become his former self again.

And so, true to his word, he took little Phil and removed to the hotel that he declared was such a well-ordered, first-class establishment.

One of the best apartments which the house afforded was neatly fitted up for him, and arranged in a way to charm the eyes of the most fastidious. A rich velvety carpet covered the floor, and a nice costly sofa stood in one corner as if to tempt the weary restless man to seek for quiet and repose upon the soft resting place. Everything else for ease and comfort was found in the room, and Mr. Payne thought, while looking around

over the various articles of utility and adorn-
ment, that he could be happy there. While
looking at the nicely bound books which lay
upon the table, he discovered a beautiful
Bible and several religious volumes; two or
three temperance papers were also seen folded
nicely upon the marble centre table.

"I wonder what Henry Weston would say
to that," he said aloud, as he was looking
over the reading matter upon the centre-
table. "I do not believe that one half the
Christian men of the town possess such a
good collection of religious books, and I do
not think that there are half a dozen sub-
scribers to a temperance paper. Mr. Freeland is a better temperance man now than
half who are so bitterly opposed to him;"
and as he settled down upon this conclusion,
a pleasant smile came over his face.

Soon little Phil came bounding into the room, his face all aglow with boyish enthusiasm, and exclaimed,

"O papa! do see what a beautiful picture book Mrs. Freeland just gave me."

Mr. Payne took the little boy's gift, expecting to find "Jack the Giant Killer," "Cinderella," or something else equally as ridiculous, but to his surprise he read upon the title page, "Child Life of Christ."

"A very pretty present, my boy," he said, the smile upon his face deepening, and fairly radiating his countenance with pleasure. "You must keep it nicely, Phil,. and you must be very good and obedient to Mrs. Freeland."

"Davie has got a book exactly like it," Philip said again, to his father.

"Then see which will keep the book the

longest time, he replied, as he started down the long stairs for the "bar-room" to speak to the landlord.

He glanced around the room half suspiciously, for just then he remembered something that Henry Weston had said about the place, but he saw nothing to make him change his ideas in regard to the gentlemanly proprietor. The walls and floor were neat and clean, and not a particle of dust or dirt could he discover upon the various articles which the room contained. Instead of the sporting pictures that are usually seen in a bar-room, there appeared nearly a dozen of fine paintings of landscape. He looked around, half expecting to find another Bible, but instead he discovered a number of temperance papers.

The landlord was a cheerful, talkative man, in middle life, and one would not term him a villain at the first sight. But yet there was an expression about his eyes that was not altogether pleasant, and a close reader of human nature might have said that he was not just what he appeared to be. But Mr. Payne saw nothing of this, and went back to his room perfectly satisfied with his new home, forgetting the warning words that Henry Weston had spoken.

CHAPTER II.

PAUL ALLEN.

PAUL ALLEN was dying — dying in the prime of life, when he should have been wearing the glorious seal of manhood upon his brow; yet he was a poor, weak, restless human being, standing upon the banks of the river, at times clinging wildly to life, and again longing to leave the world. Two years before he had been led across the border lines of the "enchanted ground," and this was the result—he was dying.

To be sure it was a short time in which the ruin had been wrought, but Paul was not one of the kind that could be held in check or kept back from the fatal goal by human hands. Yet he was not indifferent to the loving appeals made to him by those who would have saved him. He loved his wife and children well, yet there were charms upon the enchanted ground that he could not resist, and so he went to ruin. Before he became " entangled in the yoke of bondage," he had been a true husband and-father, and for many a year a sweet, deep peace had filled the old home. But after he fell, strange dark shadows came into the earthly Eden, and the flowers of hope and love faded. The sunshine went out of the once quiet home, and darkness entered. It was the old, old story of midnight watchings—of scalding tears and earnest prayers. Yet there was one uncommon feature about it— Paul Allen was never unkind or cruel to his wife and children, even when intoxicated. He was like a demon to others, warlike and revengeful, but quiet and gentle when in the home circle. People wondered at this, but failed to understand the mystery.

Disease at last fastened itself upon the once strong man, and after awhile it brought him down into the dark death valley. For several weeks he had been confined to his bed, growing more feeble and emaciated every day. For awhile the demon of appetite tortured him with its terrible power, but as he grew weaker and unable to move, it left him in some measure, and he became more like his former self. Then he saw himself as he really was, and a deep remorse came over him, with its accusing power. Poor fellow, he could only moan and weep over the wasted years, and his sad downfall.

The death-angel came for him one beautiful summer day, while his wife and two sons
stood by his bedside.   All were weeping, for
it was impossible to stand by the wretched
sufferer and not weep at the touching scene,
yet they had never ceased to love him, in
spite of his degradation, and the shame and
misery which he had brought upon them.   It
was not an easy task to forget the beautiful
life they once lived, ere he fell.

"I have got to the 'crossing-place,' Mary,"
the dying man said, as he opened his eyes to
catch another look at the faces of his loved
ones.   "It is better that I should go, I
know," he continued, "but when I look back
upon the bright years of our early married
life, I almost wish that I could live them
over again."   But here a frightened look
came over Paul's face, as he went on.—"No,

no! I would not live my life over again, for the suffering of the last two years I would not bear the second time for an eternity of happiness. Hell itself, I know, cannot be any worse in the future life than the earthly one has been through which I have passed. Poor Mary, I did not mean to treat you thus, when I stood so proudly by your side that blessed June morning and promised to love and protect you through life. But I was tempted, Mary, and fell, because I did not know the strength of my enemy—I did not know how weak I was, until I was bound by my foe. Don't blame me too much, Mary; forgive me, as far as possible, for I sometimes think that God has forgiven me. If he has, and if we should meet somewhere in the future life, you will understand it better then. Kiss me once more, Mary,—just as you used to do before the dark days came. I think that we shall meet again, for God is very merciful to such as I am."

Here Paul stopped for a moment, and his face grew strangely white, but he spoke again in a deep, husky voice.

" Howard, don't ever go to Freeland's, for there was where I yielded to the tempter. I should never have entered the doors of the other places of ruin, but it is different there, you know. Howard, promise me that you will never go there, and you too, Harry."

"I will promise, father," said Howard, in a firm voice.

Paul heard these words, and a grateful look came over his face ; and then, as he glanced at Harry, the same deathly expression appeared upon his countenance, and in a moment he was dead !

"Paul! Paul!" the poor wife moaned, kissing again and again the white face. But the dull dead ears heard not the piteous call, for they were forever closed to all earthly sounds! Poor weak, frail Paul Allen was at rest at last, and beyond the reach of human bloodhounds.

He was gently borne away to the green graveyard, to sleep in peace, while the long years should go by upon their silent wings.

"He drank himself to death," was the popular verdict of the village, and all said that the wife, children, and world at large, would be better off now that he was dead. Poor Paul was also better off.

No one thought, unless it was Mr. Weston, that Andrew Freeland had anything to do with the death of Paul Allen. Alas, how blind human beings are!

Howard Allen was an intelligent, active boy about twelve years of age. Harry was two years younger, yet he was nearly as large and strong as his brother. He was a bright, promising boy, possessing his father's yielding, impulsive nature, and the same loving, trusting spirit.

" You must watch very closely over Harry, Mrs. Allen, or he will stumble into some of these hidden pitfalls all along the pathway of the young ;" said Mr. Weston, one day, to the mother.

" I think our boys are safe in regard to intemperance, at least," replied Mrs. Allen ; " the sad lesson that they have received, I trust, will make them forever shun the path of the drunkard."

" They would not intentionally seek to walk in it, but there are many ways that lead to it, of which the young are not aware. Many a deep pitfall is covered over with flowers, and the victim is entrapped before he knows it. The devil is very sly and artful in his work of leading souls to ruin. Paul could not have been led astray in any ordinary way, for he would have fled in disgust from temptation as it usually presents itself. But there are gilded man-traps erected along the ways that lead to ruin, and they often deceive wiser men than Paul Allen."

A troubled, anxious look came over the mother's face, and so Mr. Weston did not say anything more.

More trouble soon came to the remaining members of the Allen family. Howard was suddenly stricken down with fever, and was soon raving in delirium. A physician was called, but he could not check the terrible disease or hold it in subjection for an hour. The poor boy suffered severely and was brought down in the misty valley where the King of Terrors reigned ; yet the pale sufferer in some way escaped the grasp of the relentless death-angel. Like a traveller who has been lost for many a day in the dark forest, and at last comes forth weary and benighted still, so did the pale weak boy come out of the valley of suffering. For many a day he appeared more like an imbecile than the bright manly boy that he once was. He was very quiet generally, and hardly seemed to comprehend his sad condition.

At last, however, the sunshine of his old life began to beam again over his soul, and in a few days perfect reason asserted its power in the hitherto darkened chamber of thought.

But just at that time Harry was stricken

also with the same dreaded disease, and the darkness returned a hundred-fold into the old homestead, for then the widow's money had became exhausted, and all means of obtaining more cut off. The strong arms of her manly boys had accomplished much towards procuring the daily food, but as they were useless now, want with grim features stared her in the face.

"What shall we do?" she said to herself again and again, as she understood her real position. But she was very careful not to say these words aloud, for it seemed too much like an appeal for aid should she repeat them to others.

Paul Allen had never possessed any property, save the little house and garden that his family now occupied. He had supported his wife and children by daily toil, and even in his degradation, whenever he chanced to possess a few dollars, he always gave a liberal share for their comfort. .Often when a week's work was ended, he would go quickly home to deposit a portion of his wages in his wife's hands, fearing, if he should visit the saloon first, that the money would be spent for liquor. Truly there was a vast amount of natural goodness in the heart of Paul Allen.

"How I wish that I was able to work," said Howard, the day after Harry was taken with the disease. "But it does no good to wish," he continued, as a half smile came upon his pale lips. "I shall not be strong enough for several days yet."

"For several weeks, you should have said, my son," answered Mrs. Allen, while a shadow came over her face.

"What are we to do, mother—the money is all gone, is it not?" asked the boy.

The mother started at the question, for she did not think that any one else had guessed her sad secret. For a moment she thought of trying to evade the question, but finally decided not to deceive the boy.

"Yes, Howard, it is all gone," she replied.

"Then my cow must be sold," the son said, in a decided tone.

A painful feeling came over Mrs. Allen, at such a suggestion, and yet she knew it was their last resort to obtain money, to be used to make her sick boy comfortable. She had thought of it before, but dared not mention it to Howard, for the cow was his property. He had worked for Mr. Weston, until he had earned money enough to pay for her, and then he said, as he proudly drove her home,

"I shall keep old 'Spot' as long as she lives."

In a day or two a purchaser came that way, aud Howard's cow was quietly sold to him for thirty dollars.

"I will work and buy another," the brave boy said, as he saw old "Spot" go away with the herd that the drover had purchased.

CHAPTER III.

THE GENEROUS LANDLORD—THE DREAM.

"WAIT a moment, Mr. Payne; I wish to see you upon business," said Henry Weston one morning, while passing along the street nearly opposite Mr. Freeland's hotel.

"O yes," cheerfully, replied Mr. Payne, who had just come out of the hotel, "I can spare an hour as well as not, either for business or pleasure."

"But I cannot spend but a few moments with you, for I must transact this same business with at least a dozen men within the time you mention. The fact is, Payne, they are in deep trouble up at Mrs. Allen's, and we must help them out of it as far as possible. Harry Allen is dangerously sick, and Howard is yet unable to leave the room, while there is not a dollar of money in the house. I found this out by mere accident, and started out at once for help. I have presented this paper to a number, and have obtained about fifteen dollars. I would like to get about fifty, if it is possible." And here Mr. Weston handed the paper to Payne.

" I do not think the men whose names appear upon this paper have given very liberally to the 'widow and fatherless,'" said Mr Payne. "Why, here is Deacon Turner's name, with only a dollar written opposite. He should have given five at least, for he is abundantly able to do so. He professes to be very good, and is a temperance man in the bargain. Surely he should do more than this for the widow of a man who 'drank himself to death.' Why do you not present this paper to Freeland, and get something worth taking? I believe that he would give more than any man has done thus far, unless it is yourself:" and saying this Mr. Payne wrote his own name upon the paper, and then gave Mr. Weston a five dollar bill, the sum that he had written down opposite to his signature.

"See here, Weston, just let me have this paper for five minutes, and I will get as much more money as you have obtained. There are a number of gentlemen in Freeland's bar-room, some of the free-hearted kind," and saying this Mr. Payne hurried back toward the hotel.

He was gone about fifteen minutes, and

then he came out with the paper, and as he returned it to Mr. Weston, he said :

"What did I tell you, sir ?" and then he handed twenty-five dollars to his friend. "Three gentlemen gave five dollars each, and Freeland *ten*, so you see that he is not so bad, after all ;" and a triumphant look came over the speaker's face.

"He has only returned a portion of Paul Allen's money to his family. If he should return it all there would be a hundred dollars or more ; but I will take this to the widow and children," and the bills were all carefully placed in the large pocket-book.

"There it is, again," said Payne, half angrily. "Your fanatical temperance notions make you forget to even appear grateful for favors. You abuse Freeland, I suppose, because he has given the largest sum of any that have written their names upon that paper."

"I did not mean to abuse the man ; I am grateful for the money, and if I said that he had returned it, I only spoke just as I thought. I am very grateful to you, also, Mr. Payne, and to the other gentlemen who have given so freely. But I must go, directly," and saying this Mr. Weston walked away.

" The strangest man that I ever saw, and yet I believe that he is sincere in the position he takes," said George Payne to himself, as he walked slowly down the street.

Poor Harry Allen lay moaning and tossing upon the bed in the little square room, just out of the kitchen. He, too, was delirious, and talked in a strange unusual way, about everything around him. Sometimes he would imagine that he was in Mr. Weston's hay field busy at work, spreading the new-mown hay or rolling it up in heaps, as he and Howard had sometimes done. Then again he would talk about the tall beech trees, just back of the meadow, and of the shining trout brook underneath. At times he would laugh in the old, happy way, and sing and shout to Howard, as he had often done in the grand beech woods. Poor boy, it was well that he could, in a measure, be unconscious of his suffering.

" Old Spot has come back, mother," said Howard, as he chanced to glance through the window, at the close of the day upon which the cow had been taken away by the drover.

" She undoubtedly ran away from the rest of the drove," replied Mrs. Allen. " Poor, old Spot, how I wish that we could keep her, but her owner will soon come after her again."

Just then there was a low knock heard at the door, and Mr. Weston was admitted.

"I have purchased the cow back again for you, Howard," he said, as he seated himself for a moment in the chair offered him.

"The mother and Howard both looked very much surprised, and then Mrs. Allen managed to say, "I do not quite understand you, Mr. Weston. We sold the cow this morning—we were obliged to do this," she explained, and a painful flush rested upon her face.

"Yes, I understand it all now, Mrs. Allen, and I should have done it before if I had only thought. I saw the cow in the drove to-day, and then I comprehended it all. I asked the owner to sell her to me, and finally persuaded him to do so. You can have her again, and Howard can work for me when he is well enough. I have also some money here for you which a few gentlemen in the village gave. I am afraid that you have already suffered for the want of it. I should have been more thoughtful ;" and placing the money upon the table, Mr. Weston went out.

Mrs. Allen and Howard were both too much surprised to say a word to Mr. Weston, for not until he had gone, did they fully understand the transaction. But it appeared a little plainer in a few moments, and then Howard quietly said, with a smile breaking over his face, " Mr. Weston is very good."

But the mother did not reply, and there was a strange, confused look resting upon her face. Howard noticed it, and asked :

"Are you not glad that we are so well provided for?"

"For my children's sake I am very grateful for this. And yet, I am very sorry to be obliged to receive money in such a way. But yet, in spite of this unpleasant fact, I feel very grateful to good Mr. Weston," and then Mrs. Allen took up the bills of money. "Fifty dollars," she said, aloud, after counting the money.

"And thirty more that we received for old Spot, and herself in the bargain," said Howard, in his old happy voice.

"I think that we can persuade Mr. Weston to take the thirty dollars. We will try, any way, for the fifty dollars remaining will be all that I trust we shall require, until Harry gets well again. But he is yet very sick, and may not get well as soon as we hope," and the shadow returned to Mrs. Allen's face.

"Who gave the money to us, mother?" asked Howard, with a boy's curiosity.

"Here is the paper that contains the names of those who gave it," replied Mrs. Allen, looking at the same.

Another confused look came over her face as she glanced at the names upon the paper, and she said, in a low voice,

"Strange that Andrew Freeland should have given the largest sum of any whose names are here."

"Did Andrew Freeland give any of that money, mother?" inquired Howard, in an earnest tone.

"Yes, ten dollars," answered Mrs. Allen.

"I would not keep it, mother; I would send it back to him," the boy said, in a decided manner.

" Why, my son ?" was the inquiry.

" Because he is a bad man, mother, and not what he appears to be. Don't you remember what father said about him, just before he died, and the promise I made to him? And father is not the only one that learned to drink there, for I know of several that never take a glass of liquor, only at Freeland's. Robert Wood learned to drink there, and he goes there nearly every day, to get a glass of wine. He says that he would not be seen in such a place as Butler keeps, or would not touch a particle of his drugged whiskey and rum. But Freeland, he says, keeps only pure liquor, such as gentlemen drink, and he could not be persuaded to give to his customers such vile stuff as Butler and Peck deal out to loafers and drunkards. But I guess that Robert's father does not know that he goes to Freeland's for wine ;" and here Howard happened to think that he had got away from his subject, and so he repeated the same words : " I would not keep the money, mother, I would send it back to him."

" Who will carry it back to him ? Will you, Howard ?" she asked, with a smile.

" No, for I promised father that I would never go there, and I'll keep that promise as long as I live ;" and a very resolute look came over the speaker's face.

" God help you, Howard," the mother said, and then she added, "I really wish that Andrew Freeland had not given a cent of the money. I do not see how Mr. Weston came to ask him to do so."

"I do not believe that Mr. Weston ever went into the hotel to see Freeland, anyway, for he don't think the nice gentlemanly ap-

pearing landlord is so good as he seems to be.
And I used to think so too, when I went
with father into the fine bar-room where only
gentlemen go, for if he had been a very good
man, he would not have taken the money that
we should have had."

"I do not think that we will return the
money to him. If he had given a hundred
dollars to us, it would not be any more than
he has taken from Paul," Mrs. Allen replied.

Just then there came a low call from the
little room where Harry lay. Mrs. Allen
went gently, and found her boy awake and
perfectly conscious. He reached out his
hand feebly toward her.

"What do you wish for, Harry?" she
asked, taking the hot feverish hands in
her own.

"I want to tell you what a funny dream I

had, so sit down a little while. It was about
Howard, Mr. Freeland, and myself. I
thought that we were all together upon the
'play ground' just back of the school-house,
and Howard and I were looking at a splendid lot of toys and other nice things that
Mr. Freeland had brought with him. I cannot tell you the names of half of them, but
there were toys looking just like birds and
squirrels, and at first I thought that they
were real. Then there were painted boats
and ships and all kinds of beautiful shells.
He soon arranged 'them all around very
nicely upon the low branches of the trees,
and some were placed on the ground. I tell
you the old school-grounds looked splendid,
and when Mr. Freeland hung up starry flags
an'd baskets of jewels in the tree-tops,
and then scattered gold coins all over the

ground before us, O mother, it was perfectly beautiful !

" Then Mr. Freeland told Howard and me, that if we would go with him, he would take us where all of these beautiful things could be found, and we could get all we wished for and bring them home with us. Howard said he did not believe it and would not go. But I did not think that Mr. Freeland was deceiving us, and so I started after him. He went through many a beautiful field and grove at first, and I was very sure that it would all come out right, and that I should get the nice things. But soon the way began to become dark and gloomy, and at last we were walking in a dismal swamp, where there were large frightful snakes and savage animals. Then all at once, Mr. Freeland turned into a strange wild animal, and sprang upon me. I tried to get away from him, but I saw a hundred more animals just like him all rushing toward me. I do not know just how I got away from them, but I soon found myself out in an open field, among the flowers, and Mr. Weston was there also, and helped me home again. I never dreamed about Mr. Freeland before, and I can't think how I happened to, this time." And here the sick boy closed his eyes and was soon sleeping.

CHAPTER IV.

ANOTHER MAN-TRAP.

"BOYS, you are getting too noisy," said Mr. Andrew Freeland, to two or three of his "wine customers" who seemed rather large to be termed boys. "There are a number of gentlemen staying here to-night, besides our regular boaraers ; some of these are within hearing, and it will not do to disturb them," and the landlord spoke in a low, familiar way.

"We are all gentlemen, Mr. Freeland," answered Luke Lewis, in an offended manner. "You seem to talk as though we were regular bar-room loafers, and the rest very fine gentlemen. If we are loafers we will go down to Bob Butler's and stay with the rest of them."

"You are mistaken, Luke," replied the landlord, in a very pleasant way. "I did not mean any such thing, but these other gentlemen are a little different from you. They are not such free-hearted, fun-loving good fellows as you are, but the grave, quiet ones, who think that it is a sin to smile. Why, Luke, there are two ministers and one Bible agent within hearing of this room, and I'll bet a glass of wine that they are all saying their prayers this moment, so you see that it will not do to be very noisy down here."

"Why did you not have them pray before they went to their rooms, so as not to spoil all our fun? You should have had family prayer, at least, if not a real old Methodist prayer-meeting."

"A Methodist pow-wow, you should have said, Luke," observed Walter Payson, with a sneer upon his lips.

"You are pretty rough upon the Methodists, Walter, being that you are one yourself, or used to be," and Luke laughed loudly again.

"It will not answer," said the landlord, again. "They will certainly hear you. Be quiet, boys, and some other time you can make up for this."

But the "boys" had been taking wine most too freely to be easily silenced, and so pretending not to hear Mr. Freeland's command, Walter Payson went on:

"I tell you, Luke, I have got over the Methodist fever. It did not hold on very long—this grand old wine that Freeland keeps broke it up, and I have not had a relapse yet. But father thinks I am all right yet, for he don't know about my visits here. I go to church every Sabbath, and I attend the Thursday evening prayer meeting regularly, and look as sober as father himself."

"You play the hypocrite, perfectly, I admit," replied Luke, "but you are a royal, good fellow, after all, that is after you have taken a glass or two of wine, to awaken your better nature. But let us have another drink, landlord. No, a whole bottle, I mean, and I will pay for it. Every landlord don't keep such wine as that, and some can't afford to have anything fit to drink. Bob Butler keeps nothing but the worst kind of poisonous whiskey and beer, and I don't believe that he ever saw any such wine as this in his life. But, hurry up, Freeland, for I'm getting dry."

"I think that you have taken too much wine already, boys," answered the landlord, slowly. "I would not drink any more to-night; if you do you will not be in a very good condition to attend church to-morrow."

"I think we know when we have drank enough," replied Walter, putting on the offended look that generally brought the landlord to terms.

Mr. Freeland smiled pleasantly again, and was undoubtedly about to compromise the matter in some way, when Mr. Payne came in, rather suddenly. Another gentleman accompanied him, that he introduced to the landlord as Mr. Winters—a friend who had unexpectedly come upon the evening train. He also, was evidently a gentleman, for his general appearance at once proved the fact. Freeland cast an imploring look at the two young men that were half intoxicated with the wine they had drank, but it did not avail anything, as they were not in a condition to heed the silent appeals made by the landlord.

"Please give us a bottle of the wine, Mr. Landlord," said Luke, in a voice that betrayed the fact he had already taken "too much," as Mr. Freeland had said.

But the landlord just then was very busy in talking with the new comers, and so did not heed the request.

"There comes John, he will get it for us," and so the request for wine was repeated to the bar-tender, who had been absent from the room for the last half hour. John caught a meaning look from the landlord, and so he started toward the "wine room," as if to get the wine.

The stranger, after a few moments of con-

versation with the landlord, ordered his supper, and a room for the night, and then passed
out with Mr. Payne.

"See here, boys," the landlord said, as soon
as Mr. Payne and his friend were out of hearing, "you can have the wine if you will go
away with it; but the fact is you are getting
too noisy, and I cannot allow you to remain
here. I must keep order, or the reputation
of my house will suffer. So take the wine
boys, and go away."

"Where shall we go?" asked Luke Lewis,
while a real angry look came over his face.

"See here, Mr. Freeland, if we are gentlemen we will be treated like gentlemen. If
we cannot remain here for a social time once
in a while, we have got through coming here
at all. Some of the gentlemen around here
have all the wine they wish for, and brandy

too, and remain up to drink it and have a
good time generally until nearly morning.
Some of your boarders up in the third story
do this very often. I could name these
favored ones, Mr. Freeland, and maybe I
shall, sometime. Then I know that there is
a certain room in this very respectable hotel,
that certain gentlemen employ occasionally
for certain purposes. If some of these ministers that are here knew just what I do, they
might not think that Andrew Freeland was
a Christian." And here the speaker and his
friend arose to go.

"Wait a moment, boys," the landlord said,
in his pleasant, persuasive voice. "Let me
explain a little more clearly."

But the young men were both too excited
by strong drink to listen to an explanation,
and so they walked rudely out of the room,

each using words too vile to be recorded.

"I am glad they are gone," said the land-lord to the bar-tender, who had just come in. "The fact is those two fellows are getting pretty wild, and we can afford to lose them. They will ruin our reputation if they keep on coming here, and cutting up as they have of late. They had better finish up their career down at Bob Butler's or Peck's, as they undoubtedly will. But I am thankful that there were not any present to witness their performances to-night, or rather to listen to their words."

John did not reply, for this occurred at a late hour, after the guests and boarders had all retired for the night, and the visitors gone to their several homes. John was very sleepy and so not very talkative.

"I wonder who the gentleman was

with Payne," said the landlord again. He evidently expected no reply, for he answered his own question. "He is somebody of distinction, for Payne never associates with very ordinary people. He is evidently a man of wealth and refinement, at least."

Here Mr. Freeland became drowsy himself, and suggested that they "shut up" for the night. So the floor was nicely swept and curtains dropped. The money in the till was taken out, and the bottles of liquor all removed out of sight, as it was a rule of the institution to allow no liquor to be placed in view upon the Sabbath. The blinds were closed, the doors locked securely, and then Mr. Freeland retired to his own sleeping room.

Walter Payson and Luke Lewis were in no condition to return home after they went out of Mr. Freeland's bar-room. And although they were half intoxicated, yet they seemed to be aware of the fact that they must find quarters somewhere else until the effects of the wine should pass off.

"If the barn was not quite so near our home, we would go there and remain to night," said Walter. "But the old man would be sure to find it out, and then there would be trouble."

"I want something more to drink," said Luke, "I'm fairly burning up with thirst. I would take a drink of Bob Butler's whiskey in a moment if it would only satisfy this burning appetite. Suppose we go into Butler's, a little while. He keeps open door all night, and we shall not get turned out into the street."

"If we can manage not to get found out,

we might go for this once. But if the old folks at home should find it out, they would take on awfully. Mother mistrusts now a little about matters, and watches my movements pretty closely. But I'll run the risk if you will, and if found out, I'll suffer the consequences. Never young but once, you know," and here Walter turned down the street toward Bob Butler's saloon.

In a few moments the young men walked into the bar-room of Bob Butler, and were a little surprised to find a dozen men yet remaining in the smoky filthy place. The new comers would have turned away in disgust under ordinary circumstances, but as it was they seated themselves near the door, to watch the general movement of things Some of the men present, were real "old soakers," in the last stages of drunkenness;

and not one in the room, but that showed
the effects of strong drink.   They were hav-
ing a general good time, as they termed it.
It being Saturday night, money was a little
more plenty than upon some other evenings.
They had been rather noisy before Luke
and Walter went in, but they quieted down
a little, for it was an unusual event for a
well-dressed intelligent man to be seen in
the filthy place.   But it did not last long, for
the whiskey spirit was abroad in the room,
and it soon began to reveal itself again.

"Spies from the goodly land," said one, in
a voice loud enough to be heard all over
the room.

"No, some of Freeland's gentlemen customers.   Glad that I am not one," said
another.

"But you used to be, Jack, and not very

long ago, either. You got too rough and loafer-like to suit Freeland, and so he sent you adrift, and some one else a little more refined took your place. That is the way with Freeland; he gets a fellow well to going doing hill, and just before he lands at the bottom, he gives you a hint to leave." And here the speaker stopped, as if fearful that he had said too much.

"Freeland is a regular old hypocrite, to make the best of him. He is very careful to go to church every Sabbath, and to keep his reputation good, but he is not any better, really, than Bob, yonder," said the first speaker.

"Shut your head, you fool, and let us have some more of that 'fourth-proof' whiskey. It is a mean business to be forever talking about a man at his back; so let us drink and forget Freeland and his failings. Fill up the glasses, Bob!"

Bob was not long in "filling them up," taking care to have two more than usual in readiness.

"See here, young men, I don't know as you will drink with us—Class No. 2, you know;—but I am not a going to slight you, and if you feel disposed to join us, we shall be very happy to have you do so. The liquor is capital, I can tell you ; it goes to the right place every time, and is not so aggravating as Freeland's wine is ;" and a glass of it was held toward Luke Lewis.

The fumes had reached him before, and awakened his thirst to a still greater degree, and almost unconsciously he extended his hand for the same. Another glass was placed in the hands of Walter Payson, and in a moment both were drained by the young men.

"Capital is no name for *that* liquor," said Luke, now, all prepared for a night's carousal. "Give us another drink all around, and I'll back the movement," he said, while a new, strange light gleamed in his eyes.

But we cannot describe the scene that followed. We draw a curtain over it, and will only say, that it was a sad one, like all others in such places, when a new victim is entrapped forever. That night was the beginning of a dark era in the lives of Luke Lewis and Walter Payson.

CHAPTER V.

SORROWING ONES—THE NEW MINISTER.

THE sweet, solemn Sabbath came, with its beautiful sunshine and holy stillness, and the spirit of love and tranquillity seemed to be reigning over all the land. The streets of A—— were all very quiet, and the good people seemed to be aware that it was a day of peace and rest. There was nothing to be seen or heard in the wide, pleasant streets, to remind one that sin and vice took up their abode in the quiet village. The faces of those that were occasionally seen in the street, bore not the traces of care and suffering, for sorrow generally hides itself, as far as possible, from the gaze of the curious, unsympathizing world.

But there was deep, heartfelt suffering, even in the quiet village of A——. There were aching hearts, and eyes dimmed with tears, in the little secluded hamlet, far away from the noisy, dusty cities, where vice and evil stalk abroad like a pestilence.

The sweet, loud voices of the church bells rang out upon the morning air, calling the villagers together to worship the great All-Father. Many obeyed the summons—some were indifferent to the appeal, while one or two remained at home, to hide in the seclusion of their rooms the tear-stained faces.

The dread certainty that her son was going to ruin, had just come, that glorious Sabbath morning, to poor Mrs. Payson. For many a long month she had feared that Walter was going wrong, and had watched and prayed, as only a gentle, loving mother can do. But that morning, just as the daylight began to gleam in the east, he—her only son, came staggering home, deeply intoxicated. No wonder the tears came in gushing streams from her faded eyes—no wonder that she moaned in piteous tones, " Oh, my poor boy ! Oh, my poor boy !"

She knew that the lines were passed, and that he her idol would go to ruin. She knew that there was no hope for him, for the Paysons, when once upon the enchanted ground, never got off again. One glorious, noble boy, had already been slain, and the remaining son was a victim in the same destroyer's hands. Three of her husband's brothers had fallen, and Mr. Payson himself had only been saved by adopting " total abstinence " as a rule of life.

Walter was up in his own room, sleeping

off the effects of the liquor that he had drank. He did not feel the soft air of the morning sweep over his brow. He did not see the beauty that rested upon the sky and earth, or hear the chiming bells, mingling sweetly with nature's melody. No, he only heard the din of loud angry voices, the horrid oaths and drunken songs, that still rang in his brains. He only saw flitting visions of bloated faces and red bleared eyes, such as haunted the den that he had visited the night before. Poor Walter ! will not these horrid sights and sounds break the charm that binds him to the enchanted grounds ?

Mr. Payson also remained at home, that day. It was seldom that his place in the old church was vacant, yet, he could not go there, while his son was at home intoxicated. To be sure, he did not weep, as did the poor mother, but yet the fountain of bitterness was full, and the strong man felt every moment that it would overflow.

" Can he not be saved—must he be lost ?" the mother said to her husband once that morning. But Mr. Payson did not reply. Indeed he dared not speak, for fear that the bitter fountain would break forth, and so he remained silent. But there was a look upon his face which said, " The boy is lost !"

There was another sad heart that morning in A——. A loving sister was mourning over a brother's downfall. The mother had slept for many a day in the village church-yard, and the brother and sister had been left alone in the world. Alone, did we say ? Perhaps not in the true sense, for the father yet lived, but he was a drunkard ! His wife had suffered, until the weary wheels of life stood still, and then brave little Ellen took up the burden, just where the mother had laid it down, and the home machinery went on, only going wrong when the father came. Luke Lewis was a noble fellow before he began to go to Freeland's   He loved the little resolute sister at home, and his strong manly arms procured for her the comforts of life.   And so the days went on—grand, royal old days, when the father was absent, until the serpent entered the second time into the home.

But Luke fell—just . where a thousand others have done. He "crossed the lines," and in a little time was going swiftly toward the goal of ruin. Yet he did not abandon the pure innocent sister that clung to him so confidingly. He could not do such a cruel deed very easily. He must take a few more steps in the wicked way, before he can do that. A very long step was taken the night he went into Bob Butler's—a few more like it, and he will be ready for any deed, even to shake off the little soft white hand that clings to his strong arms.

How Ellen wept that morning, and how she moaned and prayed, never can quite be told. He did not go home as Walter Payson had done, for he was too much intoxicated to walk, so Ellen, who had remained up watching for him nearly all night, went out to find the wanderer.

"Down at Butler's," some one had said to her, who had heard the sad story. In a moment the truth flashed over her mind, but she said : "Not there—not there !"

She went there. however, and inquired for her brother. In a very pleasant voice the

landlord informed her that her brother " was
in the bar-room, but was engaged just then—
would soon be at liberty, and then return
home."

"But I must see him now," she said, her lips
quivering with emotion. Bob Butler saw
that she would not be denied, and so he
said :

"I will go in and speak to him. Wait
here, and he will soon be in."

The landlord started for the bar-room, but
instead of waiting in the dingy hall into
which she had been admitted, Ellen went
softly toward the place where she knew her
brother was. The landlord had left the door
slightly ajar, and as Ellen glanced into the
room, she saw Luke trying to rise from the
floor, where he had evidently been asleep.

There was a wild, confused look upon his

face, yet his sad appearance did not prevent
the sister from springing to his side, and
winding her arms around his neck. "Luke,
Luke!" she sobbed, "why are you here?"

"Where am I?" he asked, looking around
the room. "Oh, I remember now;" and a
look of shame came over his face.

"But this is no place for you, Nell," he
said, rising to his feet.

"Nor for you, Luke," she said, looking
around the place. "It is not a fit place for
swine to live in," she added, in a firm voice.

"We will go home, Nell," the brother said,
walking in an unsteady way toward the door.

The sister was glad to get the loved one
away from the vile place; although it was a
sad blow to the pride of the proud-spirited little woman to be seen upon the Sabbath-day,
with her brother in such a condition. But

the wounded, loving heart bore a still deeper blow than pride had suffered. When safely at home, Luke also retired to rest, for his head ached sadly, and he needed more sleep. Ellen helped him to his room, arranged his bed for him, and left him alone while she went away to weep.

It was always very quiet and orderly around the hotel of Andrew Freeland, upon the Sabbath. A drunken man was never seen there, and it was very doubtful whether a drink of liquor could have been obtained in the ordinary way. The landlord was careful to walk in the path that the law had marked out for him, in this respect, and it would have been a hard matter to have proved that he had ever stepped over its limits.

At the usual hour that morning breakfast

was in readiness, and the guests and boarders all summoned to the large dining-room. Everything was in perfect order, for Mrs. Freeland was careful to maintain her reputation of being a model landlady. Travellers all said that Mr. Freeland excelled in setting a good table, as well as in maintaining order and quiet about the hotel.

"You have a very pleasant village, Mr. Freeland," observed one of the ministerial gentlemen, after the breakfast was eaten.

"Yes, a pleasant village, and pleasant people," answered the landlord. " We have but a few immoral people in our vicinity. Indeed we feel a little proud of our village and people."

" How is it in regard to the *religious* sentiments of the people?" inquired Mr. Winters.

" Morality is good as far as it goes, we often

hear said, which I believe is a **true saying.** .
But it does not always save people from sin,
although it keeps them from committing very
great offences, generally."

The landlord looked at Mr. Winters, and
the thought occurred to him, that this gentleman was the new minister that was expected
that very day in A——.   He was almost sure
of it, as he saw two of the official members of
the church in which he was to preach, coming slowly toward the hotel.

"Our churches are generally well filled,
and if that makes them religious, then they
must be so," replied Mr. Freeland, with **a**
smile.

Mr. Winters also smiled at the remark, and
replied that "bad men sometimes went to
church, while good ones remained at home."

Just then the two men who were looking

for the new minister came in, and after shaking hands with Mr. Winters, one of them inquired,

" Why did you not find the way to some of our homes? My wife was expecting you, and supposed that you would come, although I was not at home to meet you when the train arrived."

" I should have done so, but I accidentally met my friend George Payne, and as it was quite late, I accepted his invitation to remain here over night. I have had very comfortable quarters, although," he added, with a smile——

" We wish to see you alone, Mr. Winters," one of the men said, " and as it will be some time before the usual church services are to begin, I think that you had better go home with me."

Mr. Winters consented to the plan, and soon the three gentlemen went out of the hotel.

" You have an orderly hotel," observed the minister to his friend.

" Yes, and an orderly hotel keeper," was the reply. " Andrew Freeland is one of the best men in the community. He attends church regularly, and gives very liberally for all benevolent objects. If he does sell a little liquor now and then, he is not such a bad fellow, after all."

CHAPTER VI.

MORE DARK DAYS—THE TEMPTATION.

THERE were more dark days in store for Mrs. Allen and her boys. They did not depart so quickly as the mother hoped they would, but still lingered around with their gloomy shadows. Harry was just beginning to amend, when Howard again was prostrated by the same disease, and for a few days they all thought that he must die. But Howard had a work to do, and so he lived. Again he came out of the valley of suffering, in the same almost helpless condition as before, and it was feared that he would ever remain an invalid ; but he slowly regained his strength, and after a while, could walk about the house ; yet it soon became evident that he would never be the same active, strong boy that he once was. Yet, as his mind and reason were still left, Mrs. Allen did'not quite despair, but hoped that her boy would in some way be able to gain an honest living in the world.

" I am afraid that I shall not be able to pay Mr. Weston for the cow very soon," he said, half sadly, one day.

" I think that he is in no hurry for the money," replied Mrs. Allen. " Perhaps you can work in some other way, yet, and earn it. You have a pretty good education, and it may be that you can put it to some prae-tical use. When you get perfectly well we will see what can be done."

" I can do light work now, and I think that I ought to be looking for a place at once. Mr. Weston could help me, and would do so very willingly, if I should ask him."

"I do not think that you are strong enough just now to work, but you may be soon ; until you are you had better remain quiet. Some way I am sure will yet open for you," and the mother spoke in a very hopeful voice.

"I wish that I could be a book-keeper in a store," Howard went on. "Silas Grey is studying book-keeping, and his father is going to take him into his store in about a year. Or if I could be an ordinary clerk I would be very glad. I mean to ask Mr. Weston if he thinks I could obtain a position somewhere in the village, if I were qualified for such a place."

"I think that I will write to your Uncle Lawrence, and see if he cannot find some light employment for you. He is a merchant.

and is doing an extensive business in a large village—a manufacturing town in Massachusetts. He employs a number of men and boys himself, and may be inclined to give you employment in his own establishment. But we will let the matter rest for the present."

The days glided along, and soon ushered in the golden autumn. The summer that had brought so much sorrow and suffering to the Allen family, went by, and left nothing but remembrances of the scenes and events recorded. The most of them were sad ones, and yet there had been a few stray bits of sunshine here and there—enough, at least, to keep alive the sweet messenger of hope in the hearts of sorrowing ones.

Harry had become strong and healthy again, but Howard was yet frail and slender.

Disease had taken hold of him so firmly, and kept him so long, that it had left his physical powers very much impaired. But he must do something, for the money that had been given to Mrs. Allen had been exhausted, and she herself was not well enough to work as formerly. The long nights of watching with her husband and children, together with the hard labors of the day, had worn upon her, and she too was almost an invalid. So Howard began to look around for something to do, but was not very successful in finding such a situation as he desired. If he had been able to do farm-work, Mr. Weston would gladly have employed him, but, as that was impossible, he must look for something that he could do. Mrs. Allen had written to her brother, but had not yet received an answer. So the dark days lingered, in spite of all that had been done to bring peace and happiness into the little home.

"Have you found a place, yet, to work?" inquired Mr. Freeland, the landlord, one morning, as he chanced to meet Howard in the street.

"Not yet," answered the boy. "But I have only just begun to look for employ-ment," he added, stepping along as if anxious to get away from the man.

"Wait a moment, my boy," Mr. Freeland said again. "Perhaps I can help you. I have been thinking of late about getting a boy to assist John and Patrick about the hotel. They have their hands full all of the time, and if I could get some one to do a portion of the light work that belongs to them, I think that it would be good policy. The work is not done as it should be many times, and things not kept in the orderly condition that I could wish. Your duties would be very light and pleasant, and yet I would pay you good wages. I think you would do well in such a position. I will give you five dollars a week to venture, if you will come."

"Five dollars a week!" how these words tempted the poor boy; and for a few moments, he was very angry with himself to think that he had promised his father that he would never go into the hotel. Five dollars a week was more than he could earn in any other way, and a far greater amount than he had dared to hope for. "Why, it would support the whole family," the tempter whispered in his ear. "Your work, too, would be very light, and you would have a great deal of leisure time," came again, in an almost audible voice, to his ears. At first the boy really thought that Mr. Freeland had said these words, but in a moment he knew that it was his own thoughts.

"Would you wish me to sell liquor?" inquired Howard, still under the tempter's power.

The landlord evidently did not expect to hear such a question, and he started slightly, and looked the boy in the face, as he answered:

"Not very often, I think, for John or myself is usually there to attend to our customers. Your duties would generally be, to do chores about the bar-room, such as sweeping the floor, dusting the furniture, bringing in fresh water, and perhaps sometimes working under the direction of Mrs. Freeland. Then another pleasant duty would be, to drive the ponies, whenever Mrs. Freeland

and Davie wishes to go out. They are very gentle, and you can easily manage them. But what do you say about accepting this position, my boy?"

"I do not know just what to do about it," answered Howard, still thinking of the five dollars a week, and forgetting all about the promise he had made to his father.

"I know of several boys," the landlord continued, that would accept this position at half the wages that I have offered to you; but I know how much you have passed through of late, and how much you need the pay. I believe in helping the poor and unfortunate whenever we have an opportunity. And then I know that I could trust you, while some of these other boys are dishonest and tricky. Your father was as honest a man as ever walked the earth, and a noble fellow."

"Yet he died a drunkard, Mr. Freeland," replied Howard, coming to his senses that moment.

The landlord started again, but regained his composure in a moment, and replied :

"Yes, Paul drank too much.   Poor fellow ! He might have lived longer if he had let liquor alone."

"If he had never touched it in the first place, he might," the boy said, his face flushing half with anger.

"But do you know where my father first began to drink liquor ?" asked Howard, looking at Mr. Freeland steadily.

There was something in the boy's look that the landlord did not like, for he dropped his head while he answered :

"No, I do not know where he began to drink."

"It was in your bar-room, Mr. Freeland; the same place where you wish me to go."

"How do you know this?" inquired Mr. Freeland, turning away from the earnest, glowing eyes. "Because he said so, sir, and he said it too when he was dying," answered the boy, and his lips quivered with emotion.

"Indeed, I did not know that your father learned to drink in my bar-room," said Mr. Freeland, turning as if to walk away.

"But he did, though," Howard answered, "and I promised him just before he died, that I would never even enter your hotel. And I never will as long as I have my senses."

Mr. Freeland was not angry, as Howard thought he would be, but instead, a half sorrowful look came over his face, as he walked away.

Howard also passed along, with the old

bright manful look resting upon his face. The charm was now completely broken, and the tempter had been driven away.

That night the long expected letter was received from Mrs. Allen's brother. It contained good news, for the writer, Lawrence Newman, had at last found a place in his store for Howard. The boy was to have an easy position with small wages, and a portion of the time for study and recreation. The letter also contained a check of a hundred dollars, for Mrs. Allen, to use until better days should come.

"I would advise you to keep Harry at home," the brother wrote, "until you get perfectly well again. If you need more money please let me know it, and I will assist you."

This letter lifted a great burden from the

mother's heart, and happiness again began to shed its light in the little home.

"I can trust my boy with Lawrence," Mrs. Allen said, one day, to Mr. Weston, "for he is a good Christian man, with a generous heart."

"You can trust Howard anywhere, Mrs. Allen. He is as true as truth itself," answered Mr. Weston, who had in some way found out how the boy had been tempted, and how he resisted it.

"Do not borrow any trouble about him." Mr. Weston continued. "He will keep the promise he made to Paul. But you had better look out for Harry, for perhaps Freeland will try him next. You cannot just tell where nor when a rumseller will strike."

"Do you think that Mr. Freeland would intentionally lead the young astray?" Mrs. Allen asked, earnestly.

"I do not know his intentions, but I know that he has done this very thing. Mr. Freeland is far better than the most of men of his profession, and yet I regard him as a dangerous man in the community. If a rumseller can be good, moral and generous, he undoubtedly is; but I do not think that these good qualities can or should cover up his great evil of selling liquor, even though it be in the form of wine, beer and good brandy. He does harm in the world, I am sure, for I have watched him for a number of years. He is very proud of the good name which he has gained in keeping a-model hotel, and is careful to maintain his reputation. He makes a great deal of money by the large run of custom that he has. If he could gain the money without doing injury to others he undoubtedly would be very glad, but he is not willing to give up the bad business of leading men astray, because he gains money by so doing. I have not much faith in the moral principles of rum-sellers, although some claim that they are not really very bad, after all."

It was very lonely in the little cottage after Howard went from home, yet it passed away in some degree as the weeks went by. His letters came often, and always were full of hopeful, cheering words.

CHAPTER VII.

MURDER.

ATE one evening in autumn, a little more than two years after the first visit of Luke Lewis and Howard Payson to Bob Butler's saloon, the startling cry of MURDER was heard in the village of A——. It was loud and shrill, and was heard by many an ear, although the most of the villagers had retired for the night. It had never been heard in A—— before, and so, of course, the quiet people were very much startled and alarmed at hearing such a cry. Many, pale and excited, rushed toward the place where the terrible cry was still ringing out upon the air of the night; and soon a large crowd had gathered around the saloon of Bob Butler, for it was there that the alarm had been given. A terrible sight met the eyes of those who stood about the door, for the landlord, Bob Butler, lay dead upon the floor, and two other men were senseless, close by, covered with wounds and blood-stains.

Three or four more, deeply intoxicated, who did not seem to comprehend what had happened, were in the room.

Only one sober man had witnessed the affray, who had vainly tried to part the combatants, but finding it impossible, had rushed to the door, and given the alarm. Before help arrived the death wound had been given, and the soul of Bob Butler went into the presence of God. The senseless men were found to be Luke Lewis and Walter Payson.

Walter had been stricken down in the be-ginning of the fight, and so the sad truth was evident that Luke Lewis was the murderer. The officers of law were soon at hand to arrest Luke and Walter, as soon as they should return to consciousness. A physician was called, who found that Luke was injured seriously, while Walter had received two slight wounds.

" He is more drunk than injured," said the rough old doctor. " Pity that he had not been killed too, for then the world would have contained two villains less, instead of one." And then he turned to Luke to see what could be done for him.

Just as they were about to remove Luke, a woman with a white, terrified face rushed into the room.

" Where is Luke — where is Luke ?" she

cried, pushing her way toward the wounded man.

"I would not go any farther, Miss Lewis," said one, trying to keep her from looking at the bloody, ghastly face.

"Don't detain me—I must see my brother," she said, and in a moment she was kneeling by the prostrate form. "Oh, my poor brother," she moaned, kissing the bloody face again and again.

"We must remove him at once," the old doctor said, "he will die if he remains here much longer;" and then the sister's arms were gently unclasped, and the bloated, disfigured form was borne away toward home.

"He must remain there until he is well enough to go to jail," the doctor said, following the still senseless man to the little low, wooden building in which he and Ellen lived.

The wounds were all properly dressed after Luke had returned to consciousness, and he was made as comfortable as possible. At first he did not comprehend anything about the terrible affray, but in a little while, he had a faint, indistinct recollection of it. He was very weak from the loss of blood, for several deep wounds had been made by the murderous knife that Bob Butler always carried upon his person.

It was very doubtful whether either Luke or Ellen Lewis fairly comprehended that a murder had been committed, and it was well for the poor sister that she did not, for her cup of bitterness was already full that night. Luke was injured deeply, and very ill, and this was enough to make her forget everything else ; for she still loved the erring one with a true sister's devotion. She did not even see the dead form of Bob Butler, or the drunken man, Walter Payson, who were both lying near Luke.

But Luke Lewis was a murderer, for a heavy blow from his strong arm had sent a human soul into eternity, and the cold dead body was then lying already dressed for the grave, in the room adjoining the one where the fearful deed was done.

Poor Luke was a murderer, and yet he knew it not. He was a murderer, and yet the thought of taking the life of a human being had never entered his mind. He would not, in his sober moments, have harmed Bob Butler for the world, but he took his life, and the sin-stained soul went into the great future life. Alas, for poor Luke!

As might be expected, the great tide of public sympathy was all cast upon the side of the murdered man, and though Luke Lewis was far more innocent in the sight of God, than Bob Butler, yet hardly any one dared to say a word in his defence.

But there was one who dared to express the truth in words, one that public sentiment could not hold in check, and that one was Henry Weston.

"The murderer is murdered," he said, after going into the room where the deed was committed. "If all of these vampires who fatten upon the life-blood of others, could meet with a similar fate, then our young men, and the community at large, would be safe. But as long as one of them exists in our midst, not one of us is safe."

No one ventured to reply to this, for they all knew Henry Weston too well for such an undertaking, and as no answer came, he went on : " Luke Lewis is not a murderer in the true sense. He was too noble once even to be compared with such a man as Bob Butler, but now you term him a murderer, because human bloodhounds followed him until they robbed him of his honor and manhood, and he, in a fit of madness, took the life of one of these, whose business it is, to murder body and soul. I tell you, gentlemen," cried Mr. Weston, in a louder voice, while a strange light glowed in his eyes, "I believe that Luke Lewis is far less guilty than any man in this village, or in the whole land, that sells liquor in any form to others. I would rather go into the presence of God, the vilest criminal that ever lived, than a rumseller of any position in life. The innocent are generally the ones who suffer the most by the accursed traffic, but in this case the guilty has fallen—

—fallen by the works of his own hands. **If** he had been in respectable business, he would never have met such a fate. I tell you, gentlemen, this is a bad business from beginning to end, and I believe the curse of God rests upon him who tempts young men with wine, beer and cider, as much as upon one who has kept such a den of iniquity as this. Our brothers are being entrapped every day, and then rush to ruin, refusing to heed the 'handwriting on the wall.' Poor Luke **is** only one of them." Here Mr. Weston suddenly stopped and walked away.

Andrew Freeland, who had mingled with the crowd, was observed to become deadly pale while Mr. Weston was speaking, and in a few moments went hastily out of the room.

Ellen Lewis could hardly be convinced that her brother was a murderer, and when at last the truth became apparent, hope at once was crushed out of the loving, trusting soul, and a deep settled grief came over the one that had watched so faithfully and tenderly over the erring brother. For two long years had she been conscious that Luke was walking the downward path, but in all this time she had never once given up the sustaining hope that he would yet lead a better life.

But faith, tears, and prayers, did not save the ·chained soul that was struggling . for freedom in the cruel rum-demon's power, for Luke occupied one of those sad conditions in life that seem many times to be beyond the reach of mercy and the gentle influences of God's love. So Luke went down, down, until he became a wreck in body and soul, feeling at times the terrible life-shame that was resting upon him, but powerless to tear himself away from the viper that made him the wretched thing that he was.

The sufferings of those long two years cannot quite be told. Want and poverty had also taken up their abode in the little home, for Luke's strong arms no longer kept the demon away, and Ellen was obliged to bear the burden alone. It was too heavy for her, and her cheeks soon lost their rosy hues and her eyes their brightness. Two years had transformed the happy laughing girl into a pale, weary woman, but this long period of time had not the power to change the true sisterly love that glowed away down in the quiet depths of the soul. She had clung to him in spite of the shame and degradation that had eclipsed the bright sun of manhood, and robbed her idol, her much-loved brother, of all that makes life so beautiful.

Poor Luke lingered for several days upon the borders of the silent death-land —only half conscious of existence itself, and never dreaming of the fearful crime he had committed. His old enemy at times beset him with its aggravating power, and then he would feebly beg for something to drink, to satisfy the burning appetite within.

A few who had known of the struggles and trials of the sister, rallied together, and gave her the assistance she needed, in caring for the sick brother. Henry Weston went to the little cottage of suffering every day, to relieve as far as possible the wants of the sick man and the wearied sister.

Slowly Luke recovered from the effects of that eventful night; and he appeared more

like a weary child than a man. His remembrances of the past were still vague and
fleeting, and if, at times, a glimpse of the
bloody affray came over his memory, it did
not remain long enough to reveal the terrible
fact to him that he was a murderer.

But the people were thirsty after justice,
and the officers of the law were impatiently
waiting to take Luke into their own hands.
The old doctor shook his head, and said it
would not answer, but it did not avail much,
for at an early day Luke was arrested.

"But you cannot take him away from
here," said Mr. Weston, in a firm voice. "You
shall not take a man in his condition to jail."

"Will you become surety for his appearance
in court?" asked one, with a sneer.

"To be sure," answered Mr. Weston, who
at once assumed the position as bail for Luke.

"You have more confidence in the fellow than I have," said one.

"There is not a man in town that I would trust any sooner than I would Luke, when he is not intoxicated," replied Mr. Weston.

"The trouble is to catch him when he is not intoxicated," was the rejoinder.

"He cannot get to any of your man-traps, at present, and the bloodhounds will not venture into the presence of his sister to tempt him," Mr. Weston only said.

"What am I arrested for?" asked Luke, in a weak voice, while a startled look came over his white face.

"For murder, young man," answered the officer, who was about to take Luke into custody, as Mr. Weston interfered.

"Who did I murder—I don't understand it," and a piteous look came over the pallid face.

"You murdered Bob Butler, in one of your drunken sprees."

"Yes, yes, I do remember it all," cried out Luke, who seemed to comprehend the whole in a moment. "But Bob commenced it first — he tried to throw me into the street, and I and Walter only meant to keep him off. Yes, I killed him — I remember it!" and here Luke gave a loud shriek and fell to the floor.

CHAPTER VIII.

THE MURDERER'S DEATH.

"THE poor fellow will never suffer the penalty of the law," said the old doctor, who had attended Luke during his illness, to Mr. Weston, a few days after the arrest. "I do not think that he will live the day out ; and if he does an hour, he will have to rally up a good deal from what he was as I just left him. It is enough to make one's heart ache to hear the poor fellow talk. You had better step over there, Weston, and see if you cannot comfort him in some way ;" and then the doctor hurried away to visit another patient.

Mr. Weston was a little startled at the

words of the old doctor, for he had thought, until then, that Luke would recover irom his illness. He had not called in to see him for two or three days, as he had been attending to various other duties. He hastened at once to the scene of suffering, and was startled still more at the sight which he saw.

Luke was evidently lingering upon the shore of the dark river, if not already stepping out upon its icy waters, and Ellen was sitting near him, in tearless silence, clasping the clay-cold hand. At times, the dying man seemed to be perfectly conscious, and then again his mind was clouded with mists and shadows. He recognized Mr. Weston as he stepped into the room, and a faint smile came over the pale face, but it soon faded out, and a sorrowful look came in its place.

"I am a murderer, Mr. Weston—so do not

come near me! Don't you know that I struck Bob Butler a blow which killed him? But he was trying to kill me, with the deadly knife that he always carried, and I got the start of him, that was all. I did not mean to murder the man, but you see I was maddened with the drugged liquor that he dealt out to me. I paid him for it, but something that I said did not please him, as he was almost drunk himself, and then he tried to throw me into the street. We had a terrible struggle, and he drew the murderous knife, and then all forethought and reason left me. So you see that I am a murderer, Mr. Weston, and I shall die upon the gallows. The fiends have been laughing and mocking over my misfortune all night; and Bob Butler has danced about my bed, for weeks, with his demon-like face, covered with blood and wounds, just as it was the last time I saw him in his own den. Strange that he should thus torment me, night and day. There he is now, at the head of a dozen fiends, laughing in the old tormenting way. Keep him off, Nell !—he will kill me with that long, hideous knife "——— And then a loud shriek came from the pale lips.

But in a moment the wild, frightened look passed away, and Luke was himself again.

"It was dream, I guess," he continued, in a weak voice. "I thought Bob Butler stood before me. Oh, when will my sufferings be ended ? Will death ever come ? Poor Nell, how I have wronged you ! But it would never have been if I had kept away from Bob Butler's. No, no, I mean from Andrew Freeland's, for it was there that this horrible appetite fastened itself upon me. I did not think there was any danger in going there, where a drunken man was never seen. But I was mistaken, for I walked right into the jaws of ruin when I began to spend my leisure moments in Freeland's gilded trap. I was caught body and soul before I knew it, and lost forever. Poor Nell, I am very sorry, for your sake. I am not worthy of your love, and I hope that you will forget me, if possible. But I am a murderer, Nell, and you cannot forget this sad fact, though you should live a thousand years. But there comes Bob Butler again! It is not a dream this time, but a terrible reality. Satan himself cannot appear any more hideous. Nell, Nell, if you were not here, I would murder him again, so that he would stay in the lowest depths of perdition where he belongs. Stand back, fiend, or I'll strike you to the earth again," and here the dying man raised his cold white hand.

"It will soon be over," said Mr. Weston, to the pale, silent sister, who remained like a statue by the bedside.

"The sooner the better," was the low reply.

Luke never spoke again, but passed away very quietly in about half an hour. Not a tear was shed by any who saw the last struggle, and not a word was said until the spirit had forever left the clayey tenement.

"Thank God that he is beyond the reach of human justice! God will judge more mercifully than man," said Mr. Weston.

So Luke Lewis was also laid away in the bright, glowing years of his early manhood, to molder in the dust of the valley, and rest beneath the terrible name—a murderer.

" This is truly a sad affair," said Mr. Payne, to his friend Weston, after Luke was buried.

" Such affairs will happen, as long as liquor is dealt out to human beings. It cannot be otherwise very well, for causes will produce effects, you know," replied Weston.

" Yes, but I hope that we shall never witness another such a scene. And I hardly think we shall, now that Bob Butler is dead."

" He has a son, however, that is old enough to keep the murderous machine in running order," said Mr. Weston.

" But you do not think the son will follow the sad business, after all that has transpired, Mr. Weston ?"

" I cannot say," was the answer. " Men do not always regard the results of the traffic as such terrible affairs, because money is gained by the business. Money, you know, has a wondrous power to transform objects in this world, and to hide the rough edges that would appear without the magic covering.

Others will continue in the business, if young Butler does not, even after knowing all these facts as they have occurred. I presume that Andrew Freeland will never have a thought about giving up the business."

"Strange that you should compare Andrew Freeland, with such a man as Bob Butler was. But I might have known it;" and a displeased look came over Mr. Payne's face.

"But why not compare him with another of his own profession, Payne? Both have sold liquor for the same object—to grow rich—and Bob Butler was no more deserving of the fate that met him, than

Andrew Freeland would be of a similar one. If the same crime is committed in different ways, I cannot see why the punishment due to one is not equally applicable to the other. As I have said before, Freeland begins the work, and these other fellows finish it up. In Luke's case, I think this was true."

"But do you really think, Weston, that Andrew Freeland **is** such a base, degraded human being as Bob Butler was? Do you think that he would resort to such things as were hourly practiced at Butler's? And would he engage in personal combat with any human being?" asked Mr. Payne, earnestly.

"No, I do not think any such thing of Freeland. He thinks too much of his own reputation to allow or engage in any such transactions. He would never allow such a ruffianly set about him as was always found in Butler's saloon. But did he not help make these fellows ruffians, when he kept open the nicely furnished bar-room, to lure them at first from the home circle? Did he not lead them where temptation first threw its deadly charms about them?"

"They would undoubtedly have passed their time in some other place more dangerous," answered Payne. "And they might have gone to ruin far sooner by frequenting some other place. Freeland, I affirm again, is not an ordinary rumseller. He keeps a first-class, orderly hotel, which you will admit is a very necessary institution. He keeps only the best kinds of liquor, and is very careful how he deals them out. He does not allow drunkards nor drunkenness about him, and it displeases him very much whenever persons use profane language, or become disorderly in any respect. He does not allow his own son to visit the bar-room, and only last week he dismissed John the bar-tender, because he was becoming intemperate. I have boarded with him for more than two years, and have never seen anything wrong about the man. Instead of going down hill in morals, and allowing things to go to ruin as many landlords do, he grows more particular in living a blameless life, and also in keeping the hotel in the best possible order. He has disposed of all the old furniture that has become worn by use, and obtained new for every. room in the house. He is continually making improvements about the premises, and you would admit yourself, should you look them over,

that everything is in perfect order. I regard. Andrew Freeland, as a model landlord
in all respects."

" And yet he will lead scores of human
beings to ruin," was the reply. " ' The devil
transformed as an angel of light,' can do
more injury in the world than when he
appears in his true character. Two years is
not long enough to test the nature of a man
like Freeland. The model landlord may yet
reveal a character to you that will appear as
fiendish as Satan himself. Wait until a score
of years shall rest upon the form of your
manly son, then you may perhaps be able to
judge your landlord rightly, if you remain
with him for this length of time."

" Which I undoubtedly shall do," broke in
Payne, in a decided voice. " It is very pleasant to live in such a home as Freeland

makes for his guests. ·I am far more happy and contented there than I could be in any other place, since my own dear wife was taken from me. I have no fears about my own son, as I have said to you before. If Andrew Freeland is suddenly transformed into a demon, I will inform you ;" and saying this Mr. Payne turned away from his friend, to greet Mr. Winters, who just then came up.

"New forces have arrived," exclaimed Mr. Payne, good-naturedly, in a moment forgetting the feeling of vexation that the words of Henry Weston had caused.

"Now look out for yourself, friend Weston, for Mr. Winters admires Freeland as a landlord, as highly as does your humble servant. We shall annihilate you at once," and Mr. Payne laughed pleasantly.

"You cannot annihilate the truth, however—that is eternal, and will rise again, although it may be trampled in the dust. But it is an unusual occurrence to see a minister of the Gospel sustaining an evil. How is this, Mr. Winters?" and there was a strange earnestness in the speaker's voice.

"I trust that I am not sustaining an evil, when I respect such a man as Andrew Freeland," answered Mr. Winters. "If all landlords were like him there would be far less sin in the world, and we should not witness such a scene as we have to-day, very often. If Bob Butler had been such a man as Mr. Freeland, poor Luke Lewis would not have met the fate he did."

"And if Freeland had been such a man as Butler, Luke would not have been caught just as he was. Bob could not at first entrap him, but Freeland could and did. There is not much fascination about such a den as Butler kept, while there is much to charm our young men within the clean, nicely-arranged gentlemen's sitting-room of Mr. Freeland. Luke drank the fine ales and wines that this model landlord keeps, and then finished up his career by drinking the drugged liquor that Butler kept."

"How do you know this, Mr. Weston?" asked the minister, earnestly.

"By my own sense of seeing; and, besides, I heard Luke acknowledge the same with his dying breath. You should have been by his bedside when he died, Mr. Winters. Perhaps if you had you would have adopted this text to-day: 'Woe unto him that putteth the bottle to his neighbor's lips.'"

A very sober, thoughtful look came over the face of the minister of God's truth, and he

did not reply.   Perhaps the truth was beginning to break over him.   Neither did George
Payne speak, for he too was a little startled
to know that Luke had attributed his death
to the wine and ales he drank at Andrew
Freeland's.

"I hope that you will soon understand
this matter rightly, Mr. Winters," Weston
continued, "for we want your assistance in
crushing the evil from our midst.   The friends
of truth and of Christianity at least should
be arrayed against the destroyer of our race.
We do not want many such convincing arguments, as we had to-day, when Luke **was**
lowered into the grave, for one is enough,"
and then Mr. Weston was suddenly called
away by a friend.

CHAPTER IX.

THE LANDLORD'S GIFT.

THE death of Luke Lewis seemed to fully arouse Walter Payson to a sense of his own wretched condition. He was greatly alarmed, and eagerly looked about him for some way of escape. He knew the destroyer was upon his track, but he did not know just how to evade him. No wonder poor Walter was puzzled to know how to save himself, for he was surrounded upon every hand by the powers of darkness, and these remorseless fiends seemed determined to devour him. And the greatest of his mortal enemies was the fatal appetite for strong drink—the same demon that had de-

stroyed so many of his race. It had been
his master ever since the day that he drank
his first glass of wine at Andrew Freeland's.
And a cruel master it had proved, for it had
robbed him of manhood—of principle, and
his hopes of heaven. It had clung to him
with more than mortal power, dragging him
downward, and writing upon his brow the
traces of shame. He did not seem to understand his true position until after the murderous affray at Bob Butler's. Like the jailor
of old, he could only say, "What shall I do
to be saved?" and the same answer came to
him at last: "Believe on the Lord Jesus
Christ, and thou shalt be saved."

"It is my only hope of salvation, I know,"
he said to Mr. Winters, who was trying to
lead the wanderer back to his Father's house,
" and yet I am afraid that even this will not

save me. You know nothing about this terrible, burning appetite, Mr. Winters."

"It is true that I know nothing about your appetite for liquor, but I do know that God's grace is sufficient for all things, as His word declares," Mr. Winters replied. "Look to Him, Walter, and He will save you. Start again for the 'golden gate,' and keep away from temptation. Do not once venture where liquor exists, until you have overcome the dreaded foe."

"I first began to drink at Freeland's," Walter said, "and it was his fine liquors that caused this cursed appetite to spring into existence. I might have known better, for father warned me, and pointed out the danger. But I did not heed it, although I knew how many of my kindred had gone to ruin. But I will try to overcome, God help me."

So Walter Payson tried to be a man again and overcome the terrible appetite. A hard struggle he had, for weeks after Luke Lewis was buried. He was confined to his bed—weak as a child, and at times moaning in delirium for something to quench the appetite within. Every nerve and fibre of his being seemed to be unstrung, and often he would weep in piteous accents, and pray to die. The very sight of a goblet, or even a bottle containing medicine, made him almost frantic, and he seemed more like a wild animal bound with chains than like a human being.

"Mother, mother, I shall go mad unless I have something to satisfy this horrible appetite that is consuming me," he said again and again. The poor mother could only weep and pray over the shattered bark that seemed about to go into the mad vortex of ruin.

But the good angel did not leave the struggling, suffering one to drift out upon the tide of death, for he was sustained by some invisible power, and kept in the narrow way that leads to Life. Very slowly he recovered from his illness, and like a pale shadow, he walked about the old homestead. He dared not go into the streets, for fear of meeting some of his old companions again, nor did he venture even in sight of any of the familiar haunts of sin, for he knew his own weakness too well, to place himself in the tempter's way.

His wan, emaciated face awakened the pity of all who chanced to behold the " living wreck " which he appeared to be, and many a kind word was whispered softly in his ear ; but while he acknowledged the kindness of his friends, the same sorrowful look remained upon his face, that was seldom lit up with a smile. But as time sped along, strength came again to Walter's arms, and the dissipated look, in some degree began to wear away. Hope also came to give peace to him, who had so long been troubled with distressing fears that he would fall again. An occasional smile would sometimes glow upon the face, and a hopeful word fall from the lips. Yes, Walter Payson was slowly gaining ground, while bravely struggling for the victor's crown.

Two or three times he was assailed by outward foes, but quickly tore himself from them and was free at last from their assaults. This was a grand triumph, and he breathed freer after this, and walked the earth with a firmer tread. But he was still weak, and not able to appear as a man among men; and yielding at last to the conviction that he must again confess Christ to the world, in order to stand, he came humbly to the altar of salvation, and was received by the loving father who met the returning prodigal, and placed upon him the "ring and robe," forgetting that he had ever strayed from home out upon the wilds of sin. The old white-haired father spoke kind, encouraging words to his son — the faithful mother watched and prayed, and friends and relatives sought in every possible way to help the young man along in the way of right and truth. Even Andrew Freeland shook hands with Walter, and bade him a friendly "God speed" in the better way.

"Look out for yourself, Payson," he said, "and don't get to going down hill again."

"Then I must not patronize your bar,"

replied the young man, a little bitterly. "I began this bad business by drinking your pure liquors, and if I would keep clear of danger, I must also keep clear of you."

A slight shadow came over the landlord's face, but he answered very pleasantly:

"I would not advise you to drink anything—not even ale or wine, for they might get you into trouble again. I am sorry that you ever touched them at all, and if I am in any way responsible for your downfall, I will try and atone for it, if possible. If you will keep perfectly sober for one year, I will make you a present of as fine a suit of clothes as can be purchased in town. And I will, moreover, promise you that you shall never be tempted to drink, should you visit my barroom again. Neither shall you have a drop of liquor if you ask for it," the landlord added, in a louder voice.

This conversation occurred in the street, where these two men had chanced to meet, and no one had heard it, only Mr. Winters, who joined them in time to hear Freeland's reply to the young man.

" A suit of clothes is worth trying for," the minister said, smiling in a pleasant way; "but there are other things that you will gain, of far greater value," he added, more seriously. " There is your health, your good name, your present happiness, and your soul, Walter; and any of them is worth a great struggle upon your part."

" They will cost me a great struggle, one that I am fearful will be greater than I can endure. Yet as I have said before, I will try. If I gain the victory I shall be the happiest being in the world ; if I fail I shall be lost forever ; " and as the young man said this, he walked away, with hasty steps.

" Poor fellow," said the landlord, in a sympathizing voice, to Mr. Winters.

" If all would adopt your position, Mr. Freeland, in regard to not leading him into temptation, he would be safe enough ; but they will not do this, but will entrap him again, if possible."

" I do not just see how they can do such a cruel deed," answered Mr. Freeland. " I would not ask the young man to drink again for the world ; and if I had known how it would have ended, I would never have given him a drop of liquor in any form. But it is very seldom that we find one constituted like Walter—one that possesses such an appetite for liquor. I generally find that wine and ales prove a barrier to drunkenness ; but he claims that these light drinks only created a stronger appetite for liquor. It is not pleasant to run the risk of making men drunkards, yet I think that if they will drink, it is better to give them something that will not harm them, as the drugged, poisonous liquors, usually do."

Mr. Winters evidently approved of the way that the landlord adopted to suppress intemperance ; knowing, however, the Bible command, that we are not " to continue in sin that grace may abound ;" and so no word of condemnation came from his lips. The man of God did not breathe a word of reproof to him who was daily leading souls in the way to ruin, but smiled approvingly upon a work that Satan rejoiced over.

" Walter will yet be the staff and comfort

of my declining years," the father said again and again, while a tear or two of happiness would gather in his dim blue eyes. "My brothers died, it is true, but my son will live, and be a man in spite of the powers of darkness which sought to drag him to ruin."

No wonder the old man was happy in believing that the son would sustain him while tottering down the western hillside of life. He needed a strong arm to lean upon, for he was nearing the plains of immortality, at the base of life's mountain—poor in regard to worldly riches, and divested of the means to provide for himself and companion.

So as the first year of Walter's new life sped away, the old father dreamed on the happy dream.

Just one year from the day that Walter had met Mr. Freeland, he received the suit of clothes that had been promised to him, if he should remain sober. He had forgotten the promise, and would never have thought of it again had he not received the large package of clothing and a polite note from Mr. Freeland, begging him to accept the present. The young man hardly knew whether it would be proper for him to return the package to the landlord or not. The clothes were an acceptable present to him, for he had had a hard struggle, even with the assistance that had been given him, to live from day to day. He had not been able to labor, only for a short time, and then he did not receive a man's wages, as he had not fully recovered from his two years' carousal.

"Keep the clothes, by all means, Walter," said Mr. Winters, who chanced to call at

Mr. Payson's the day upon which they were received. "Mr. Freeland is a kind-hearted man, and wishes to encourage you onward in the path of right. He has often inquired after you, and expressed a desire that you would continue to live a sober life. He is a better man than many of those who profess to be Christians, so accept his fine present, my boy, and keep on living the nobler life."

CHAPTER X.

ANOTHER VICTIM.

"AND so Harry is at work for Mr. Freeland," said Henry Weston, one day, to Mrs. Allen.

The mother's face flushed deeply, as these words came to her ears, but a sad, pained expression soon came over it.

"I could not help it," she replied, in a low, unsteady voice.

"It is cruel as the grave," Mr. Weston continued, "for Freeland to get the boy into his clutches. It was bad enough for him to ruin Paul without trying his skill upon the son."

"But he has not ruined Harry yet," Mrs. Allen said, quickly.

"Not yet, to be sure. It takes some little time to torture one to death. It is better to kill outright. But he has begun the work, Mrs. Allen, and it will not take long to finish it upon such a boy as Harry. He will not last so long as his father did."

"But what can I do?" asked Mrs. Allen, excitedly.

"Get him away from there, if possible."

"It is not possible, I am afraid," replied Mrs. Allen, sadly. "Harry is resolute and headstrong, and will not listen to reason. Had it been in my power to prevent him from going to Mr. Freeland's he never should have gone. But the truth is, he was very anxious to get the position, after hearing Mr. Payne express his opinion of the landlord, and tell of his kindness to all that he employed."

" And Freeland was just as anxious to get Harry as he was to go. He always watches for good game, and your boy will suit him exactly. Harry is quick, handy, and intelligent. And then he wants a boy that he can lead about just as he pleases, and make him believe whatever he teaches. Harry is easily. led, as the landlord well knows."

"I have been in hopes," said Mrs. Allen, " that the charm would wear off in a little while, and that he would come home again. But I see no signs of it yet."

" And you never will, I am afraid. The charm about liquor and the place where it exists never wears off. The boy will go to ruin if he remains there."

" I am afraid that it will not be much better if we succeed in getting him away. He is restless and uneasy at home, and I think that he would not remain long here at the best. I wish that Harry was as good and obedient as Howard," and here the face of the mother flushed painfully at the confession that Harry was not so kind and noble as his brother.

"He will be obedient to Mr. Freeland, however," Mr. Weston replied. " It is strange how much easier it is to lead one in the wrong way than in the right. But we must devise some way to get Harry to return home again."

" I will go and see Mr. Freeland myself," said Mrs. Allen. Perhaps he will heed the request of a woman. I will ask him to find some one else, and let Harry come home again."

" Perhaps you will succeed, but I doubt it. Mr. Freeland will appear very kind an I

gentlemanly to your face, and make all manner of promises, and deceive you if possible. Don't believe all that he says, Mrs.
Allen," and saying this Mr. Weston went
away.

True to her word, Mrs. Allen visited the
hotel and requested to see Mr. Freeland.

" I called to speak to you in regard to
Harry," she said, after she was seated in the
nicely furnished ladies' sitting-room.

"All right, Mrs. Allen," he replied, in a
pleasant voice. Harry is a fine boy—the very
best that I have ever employed. He is worth
a dozen like John Hall, the fellow that formerly filled your boy's place."

Mrs. Allen was conscious of a feeling of
pride coming over her at these words, and
for a moment she half regretted that she had
come upon such an errand. But remem-

bering Mr. Weston's advice, she finally managed to say :

"But I would rather Harry would not remain here"——

"Why, my good woman?" inquired the landlord, in a surprised tone of voice.

"I am afraid that he will contract bad habits if he remains here. He is at just the right age, you know."

"There is not the least possible chance for it, Mrs. Allen," answered Mr. Freeland, with an assuring smile. "Your son is just as safe here as he would be in the family of Mr. Winters himself. I do not allow demoralizing influences to exist here. The fast young men of our village do not visit us, as they do not meet with a very cordial welcome. I allow no profanity, and in fact, nothing that can injure the moral character of your son. Indeed I think that he is as safe as he would be in your own society."

"But you sell liquor, Mr. Freeland," said Mrs. Allen. "There is where the danger lies. Paul, you know, could not let liquor alone"—and here a sigh came from the speaker's lips.

The landlord started slightly at these words, and for a moment the pleasant smile departed, but before he answered it returned.

"I do not think that there is any danger in this respect, Mrs. Allen," he said. "Harry is not constituted just as Paul was, and will not fall into temptation as readily. And then my liquors are not so dangerous as the vile compounds found in the most of hotels. I keep only pure wine, ale and brandy of the very best quality. I never sold a drop of drugged liquor in my life."

"But even these kinds of liquors make drunkards. Paul, you know "——'

"Don't borrow any trouble about your son, my good woman," Mr. Freeland said, suddenly interrupting her. "I will look after the interests of Harry, and he shall not have anything to do with the liquor. There is enough for him to do without meddling with it. He works under the direction of Mrs. Freeland a large portion of the time, and I do not think that she will lead him into temptation. But here he comes now, as happy as a king," and Mr. Freeland pointed through the open window, where Harry could be seen driving the landlord's gray ponies.

Mrs. Allen glanced at the manly form of her son, and noted the happy, joyous expression upon his face as he reined up the prancing ponies in front of the door. He had not

been at home since he began his work at Mr.
Freeland's, for he went without his mother's
consent, and even when she did not know
it. She was generally considered to be a
weak, yielding woman — one who would sub-
mit to a wrong, rather than to lift her hand
against it. But as she had suffered so deeply
through the ravages of intemperance, she
had indeed tried to keep the monster away
and save her two boys. She had talked and
reasoned with Harry until she was convinced
that words would avail nothing, and then
she gave up the contest, just where she
should have used parental authority in de-
manding obedience. But she failed here, and
Harry went to live with the smooth-tongued,
wily landlord who had drawn the boy into
the gilded trap.

Mr. Freeland went out of the room, to assist his wife as she alighted from the carriage, and Mrs. Allen remained to speak with Harry. The landlord had half convinced her that Harry was not in danger, in spite of the knowledge that her husband had taken his first steps toward ruin in the same place where her boy was to remain.

Harry sprang from the carriage and entered the large open hall, singing a little hymn that he had learned at home. The door that led into the sitting room was open, and so he saw Mrs. Allen as he came along. The happy look faded away in a moment and the singing ceased, for he evidently guessed his mother's errand. But yet he entered the room and reached out his hand, which was grasped by the indulgent mother. He was dressed in a suit of new clothes, which Mrs. Allen had not observed before.

" Mr. Freeland gave them to me," he said, in answer to her inquiring look, " and he gives me five dollars a week, and it is nothing but fun to work here. Next Saturday night I shall bring every cent of my wages to you. I have not spent a cent yet, and Mr. Freeland promised me another suit of clothes at the end of the year, if I would carry my wages all to you. He furnishes me with candies and nuts, as he has plenty of them."

" Do you have anything to do with the liquors ?" asked Mrs. Allen, in a half eager voice.

" Nothing but to wash and rinse the glasses occasionally," he replied, a little reluctantly.

A shadow came over the mother's face, and she said :

" If you did not have this duty to perform, I should feel safer."

"Which he shall not," said Mr. Freeland, as he came in just in time to hear the remark.

A look of relief came over the face of Mrs. Allen, which the quick eye of the landlord saw.

"I assure you again," he went on in a bolder voice, "that my hotel is very different from others that are called hotels. I am trying to begin a reform in this direction, for to tell the truth the most of landlords are too slack, and keep low drinking saloons instead of orderly places of rest and repose for travellers. I strive to keep a model hotel in every respect, and people generally think that I succeed. Ask Mr. Winters or Payne, who has boarded with us for three years."

"I am convinced that you are not like the most of landlords, but I was afraid that my son would learn to drink, as his father did.

Paul did not drink liquor until"—and here Mrs. Allen stopped as she noted the unpleasant look upon the landlord's face.

"Don't borrow any trouble about the boy. I will watch him closely, and I repeat the promise to you again, that he shall not touch the glasses again or have anything to do with the liquor."

Here the landlord was called away, and Mrs. Allen also went out of the pleasant sitting-room. A great burden had been lifted, and she breathed more freely as she returned home. Alas, she too had become charmed by the glitter of the serpent's eyes.

CHAPTER XI.

THE MINISTER'S VOW.

"THE blood of our blessed Jesus," said Mr. Winters, in a low thrilling voice, as he stooped to place the silver cup of wine, representing the blood of the world's Redeemer, to the lips of Walter Payson, who knelt at the altar, for the administration of the Lord's Supper.

The young man became deadly pale, and trembled violently, as he took the sacred cup, which would have fallen to the floor, had not Mr. Winter's hand also been upon it. He made no movement toward placing his white lips upon the edge of the silver cup, and so

Mr. Winters continued : "Drink this in re-membrance that Christ's blood was shed for thee."

But yet he did not taste of the red wine. The minister placed it closely to the ashen lips, while he repeated, "May His blood pre-serve thy soul and body unto everlasting life."

"This will ruin my soul and body," the young man tried to say, but the words died out upon his lips 'as the cup was pressed against them. He could not resist any longer, and so he drank the wine, instead of tasting it, as Mr. Winters intended. The cup was instantly taken from his hand and passed to the next, but it was too late. The life-blood rushed swiftly through the veins and arteries of Walter Payson, and a mist was before his eyes as he rose to his feet. He managed to go back to his seat and sink like a wearied child upon it ; yet the terrible spell was upon him and he was lost. Every eye was upon him, and nearly all in the church wondered what it all meant. Only two or three guessed the true cause, and one of these was Mr. Weston, who was almost as pale and excited as Walter himself. Others gathered around the altar to partake of the bread and wine—emblems of the body and blood of the blessed Saviour—and the sweet voice of prayer and praise blended softly with the scene.

The tones of the loud organ pealed out at last, filling the old church with melody, but poor Walter Payson was unconscious of it all, for he neither saw nor heard aught of the holy scene. The dark tide of agony was rushing over his soul, and he felt that he was drifting out upon the moaning ocean, where phantom ships freighted with cruel demons were all about, waiting to devour him. He tried to pray, but his thoughts were strangely confused, and he forgot the simple form of prayer—for the awful, burning thirst was upon him—devouring and consuming his very soul. Hell itself could not have been worse than the tortures that he endured, and in his agony he rushed from the church toward the nearest drinking saloon. It was the very place where Bob Butler was murdered, yet this knowledge did not stop him or even arrest his steps for a moment.

"Give me something to drink, for I am burning up with thirst," he said to the startled bar-tender, who was sitting near the door, half-stupefied with liquor himself.

"What did you say, sir?" he asked, staring

at Walter, and rubbing his eyes to know whether he was dreaming or not.

"Liquor, you fool!" the new comer demanded, in tones that the bar-tender understood.

" Yes, yes, Payson, all right—I'll get it in a moment," and the fellow started for the bar.

" Be quick, sir, or I'll help myself," Walter said, in a loud voice.

In a moment more he had drained the glass of liquor placed in his hand by the willing bar-tender, and then there was a stranger, wilder look than ever in his eyes. It did not satisfy the terrible appetite, however, but increased it with two-fold power. He was almost frantic with the burning pain that was sweeping over him.

" More," he only said, while he reached his hand eagerly out for another drink.

It was like placing wood upon the fire, for the vile compound only increased his appetite to a still greater degree. After he had drank two or three glasses more, and sat down upon the bench close by, the door was pushed open and Mr. Winters and Weston entered.

"I told you that we should find him here," said Mr. Weston to his companion.

The minister's face was as white as snow itself, as he advanced toward Walter and grasped him by the arm.

"What does it all mean, Walter?" he said. "Surely you have not been drinking!"

"But I have, old fellow," broke in the half drunken man, laughing in a strange, unusual way. "I have been taking some prime 'old rye,' and if you don't believe it, just take a drink yourself. I say, Tom, just turn out the minister a drink, and I'll make it all right with you.   Ha, ha, wont it be fun to drink with the Rev. Mr. Winters? Do you hear, blockhead, or be you deaf?"

"Come away, Walter," pleaded Mr. Winters, who grasped the trembling arm more firmly.

"No, siree! Rev. Mr. Winters, you don't do it.   I'm not going back to church, where I can only just taste of your choice wine, that you got of Andrew Freeland.   It is too choice for me, and I shall not touch it again. But come, take a drink of this, and then we will all go up and hear you preach this evening.   I tell you, it is capital"——

"Come Walter——do not remain any longer. Come, and I will go home with you," urged Mr. Winters.

"I shall not go just yet, Mr. Minister.   I have concluded to remain here a day or two, and when I do go I can go without any of your help. So just trot along, if you are not going to drink: I can drink it, if you do not;" and saying this Walter grasped the empty glass which was within reach.

Again the door was pushed open, and a gray-haired man entered, trembling with emotion.

"Walter, Walter, come away," he said, as he hastened toward his son.

"Sha'n't do it, old man," Walter replied, in a thick, maudlin voice. "I've got out from under your thumb, and ain't going back again. Just fill up that glass again, Tom."

"God help me!" exclaimed the old man, leaning against the bar for support, and then the tears ran down his wrinkled face like rain.

Mr. Weston approached the old man, and

taking his arm, tried to help him away from the unholy place. But the poor, unhappy father could not stir, but remained upon the seat, weeping and moaning like an infant.

"Dry up, old man, and don't snivel like a baby," Walter said, staggering toward his father. But it was doubtful whether the old man heard these words, for he seemed to be unconscious to all things, save his own bitter sorrow.

"Walter, my son—my son," he only said, as the fierce storm swept over.

"This is no place for Christian men," Mr. Weston said, again trying to lift the old man to his feet. Mr. Winters grasped the other arm, and together they bore him home.

"This is terrible business," said Mr. Weston, as they walked away from the home of Walter Payson.

"Yes," answered the minister, in a low voice, and then he added, "I did not think that there was a man in the world constituted as Walter Payson is."

"There are thousands of them," answered Mr. Weston. "And I think we ought to be very careful how we lead them into temptation. It is not safe to use the hateful poison in any way, not even in remembrance of the sufferings of our Saviour. It is a terrible mockery to use this liquid of damnation, to represent the blood of the world's Redeemer."

"I never looked at this matter in such a way before," Mr. Winters said.

"Truth is truth, let us view it as we may," was the answer.

"I shall never use any intoxicating beverage again, to represent the blood of our Saviour," said Mr. Winters, in a slow, decided voice. "This day's experience has proved to me that it is not right to do it, and I am willing to live up to my convictions of right and duty. I make this vow voluntarily, fully convinced, that I have committed a great error by placing it to the lips of Walter Payson."

"I am glad that you see your duty in this respect," answered Mr. Weston, "and I hope that you will understand the true principles of temperance, in every way as well. Total abstinence is the only safe rule of life, and any one who violates this one great law of God and nature, is certainly a transgressor."

"If I have sinned in this respect it has been done through ignorance," acknowledged Mr. Winters. "Had it not been for this day's lesson, I should undoubtedly have believed in the future, just as I have in the past."

" Human beings are sometimes very slow to receive the truth," was the quiet answer. " Some might have been convinced of it in regard to using alcohol in any form, without the sad lesson of to-day. But I hope that you will not wait to receive such a lesson, before you discover the evil that Andrew Freeland—the model landlord—is doing."

Mr. Winters started as this name came to his ears, and a deep flush came over his face.

" You obtained this very wine which has made so much trouble to-day, of Mr. Freeland, and it cannot be any safer for him to give it to others than for yourself. It is true that Walter would not have gone there for wine, but others will go and be ruined. It was Freeland's wine that has twice dragged Walter down. Once he took it in the model hotel, and once at the communion altar.

Both times it led him into sin, and this proves that it is not safe to give it in any way."

Light seemed to be breaking over the soul of the minister of God, and large drops of perspiration stood upon his forehead.

"I'll walk in the light, as God shall give it to me," he said, in the same firm voice.

"Amen," was the answer.

CHAPTER XII.

LITTLE PHIL.

"WHAT is the matter with little Phil?" asked Mr. Freeland, one afternoon, as he entered the nice, tidy bed-room which was occupied by the landlady.

"I do not know," answered Mrs. Freeland, in a somewhat anxious tone. "He has behaved very strangely since dinner, and I do not know just what to make of it. First he laughed, danced and sang in a strange, unusual way, and then he complained of feeling sick."

"Where has he been, and what has he

been doing ?" asked the landlord, in an un-steady voice.

"He has not been anywhere,—not even out of the house, to my knowledge. He and Davie have been playing together in this very room for the last two hours."

"Where is Davie?" asked Mr. Freeland, again, in a hasty voice.

"He has just gone to his room, for his afternoon nap," was the answer.

"Does Payne know that Phil is sick?" again asked the landlord.

"No, he is out somewhere. We had bet-ter send Harry after him," and saying this Mrs. Freeland started for the door.

"No, no, don't send for him, for heaven's sake! I would not have him see Phil in such a condition for the world. The boy is drunk, Mrs. Freeland."

The landlady started at these words, and then a deep flush came over her face. She looked at her husband in an inquiring way, only saying : " Impossible !"

"But it is possible, Mrs. Freeland," he said in reply, "and now I shall find out how it happened," he added, as he arose and went to a cupboard in the wall of the room. He opened the door and saw one empty wine bottle, and two about half full.

" Just as I expected, Mrs. Freeland. The boys have been helping themselves to your wine. I should hate to have Payne find it out. Keep the boy out of sight, if possible ; and then he walked hurriedly out of the room. Just then Mr. Payne came in to the large hall, and inquired for his son.

" He is somewhere around the house," Mr. Freeland replied, in an evasive voice. " No,

I am mistaken," he added, as if recollecting himself. " He and Davie have gone into the woods for nuts. They will be back soon, however, I guess."

" I am sorry," answered Mr. Payne, " for I wanted Phil to go with me. I had planned an excursion into the woods, but it will be too late when the boys return, undoubtedly."

Mr. Payne stepped along into the sitting-room, and just at that moment little Phil called wildly out to him. The strange, un-natural tones of the boy startled Mr. Payne, and he rushed toward the bed-room door.

" You here, Phil !" he exclaimed, as he saw his boy so pale and lifeless upon the bed "But what does it all mean? Are you sick, Phil?"

The boy attempted to rise, but fell like

a log back upon his pillow, while the wide, staring eyes were fixed upon his father.

"Go for the physician, Harry," Mr. Payne shouted, in a commanding tone. The order was quickly obeyed, and in a few moments the old doctor was bending over the pale-faced boy. He made a few inquiries of Mrs. Freeland, glanced again at the patient, and then took his hat and medicine case as if to walk away.

"What do you mean?" inquired Mr. Payne, in a surprised way.

"I mean that I am going away," he replied, indifferently.

"But why don't you do something for my son?" the father asked, excitedly.

"I can do nothing for him, Mr. Payne. Yet I might as well tell you the truth, your boy is drunk;" and the rough old doctor walked away.

"It cannot be," the father groaned. "The doctor is mistaken;" but suddenly remembering how Mr. Freeland had tried to deceive him, he stopped.

"Tell me, woman," he said, turning to Mrs. Freeland, "how this happened?"

"I do not know," she said, trying to turn away from the half glaring eyes of the father.

"Yes, you do know. Don't try to deceive me, for I will know the truth of the matter. Where did he get the liquor he drank?"

The landlady knew something about the determined disposition of Mr. Payne, and she saw in a moment that it would not do to try to deceive him.

"He must have got it out of the cupboard yonder," she at last confessed.

"I did not know that you were in the habit of storing your liquor around the house in such a way. I supposed that you kept it in the liquor-room, guarded by a lock and key. I shall examine my own room to see if there is any secreted there ;" and here Mr. Payne stopped.

" It was some that I kept here for my own use," acknowledged the landlady, trying to explain the matter a little better.

" I did not know before that you had any particular use for liquor ;" and saying this, Mr. Payne took little Phil in his strong arms and bore him to his own room.

The boy did not awake until the next morning, and then he was dull and spiritless. It was a long time before he could remember anything about the transaction of the previous day, but at last it all became clear in his memory.

"What made you drink the wine, Phil?" Mr. Payne asked.

"Davie gave it to me," the boy answered, a little confused.

"Did you ever drink any before yesterday?" was the next question.

"O yes, lots of times; Mrs. Freeland always gives it to us when we take our lunch in her room, with her. She says that it will not hurt us, if we do not take too much. But I guess that we did drink too much yesterday, for it made me feel so strangely, and then my head ached badly."

"What made you get it yourself?" Mr. Payne asked.

"Because Mrs. Freeland did not give us all we wanted. It was so nice and sweet— and then we did not think that any one would know it."

A long talk followed this confession, and much good advice was given to the little tippler. He was forced to promise that he would never meddle with liquor again, although he did this very reluctantly. His acknowledgment that he loved the "nice, sweet wine," troubled Mr. Payne more than the knowledge that his son had been intoxicated. The smiling landlord made many apologies, and then reluctantly stated, as he affirmed, that the physician had prescribed wine for Mrs. Freeland. He was very sorry that she had been so indiscreet as to offer it to the boys, but he would talk with her at once in regard to the matter, and such a thing should never happen again. Nobody knew anything about the transaction but themselves and the old doctor, and he would see him at once, and the matter should be kept secret

Mr. Payne did not really like the way the affair was to be settled, for he hated deception, but he did not just see what he should do, if he should go away from Mr. Freeland's, and so he listened to the voice of the tempter and concluded to remain. He did not feel exactly satisfied with his decision, yet he reasoned that Phil was old enough to listen to reason, and that he would watch over him very carefully in the future. And then he was sure that the landlord felt almost as badly over the affair as he himself, and would also guard against its repetition, Thus the still voice that bade him go away from Mr. Freeland's was quieted, and the man dreamed on. But the awakening will come, ere long.

CHAPTER XIII.

A CRUEL LESSON.

WALTER Payson did not go back to his father's house humbled and penitent, after the events of that Sabbath day. As reason again resumed its power, after the effects of the liquor wore off, a strange despondency came over him, and he seemed lost to all emotions that were pure and good. Mr. Winters had hoped that the young man would see his great error—make a full confession of his sin, and return to the ways of right and sobriety. But he was mistaken in supposing that Walter would do this, for the poor victim of error was lost in the wilderness of hopelessness and despair. And then the terrible appetite was upon him, binding him body and soul, upon the lowlands of shame and wretchedness. Weak and powerless, he yielded to be led farther into the paths of sin, and never once lifted his weak arm against the strong foe. Swiftly he rushed along in the way of ruin.

But it was more than the poor old father could bear, and from the day that Walter fell, he never appeared like himself again. Reason seemed to leave him, and like an idiot, he wandered around, talking to himself in a sad, plaintive way.

Sometimes he seemed to partially understand it all, and then he would pray to die. His prayer was answered at last, for suddenly one day, the wheels of life stood still. He was buried in the village church-yard, and as Walter stood by the open grave, he appeared as indifferent and unconcerned as the unfeeling saloon-keeper himself, who also was near. There was no expression of sorrow upon the young man's face, no look of regret or tenderness, nothing but a vacant stare, which told of the darkness within his soul. He did not seem to hear the low sad moans that came from the lips of the poor old mother, who was trembling with grief and emotion. Indeed he appeared as devoid of all feelings of sorrow and tenderness, as the rocks of the mountain.

"Go home with your mother, Walter," Mr. Winters whispered in the ears of the son, as they were all preparing to leave the church-yard. But Walter did not seem to hear these words, for he turned indifferently away, and walked toward the saloon.   Before night he was deeply intoxicated, and slept off the effects of the drugged liquor in the low filthy place where he drank it.

The weeks passed swiftly along, bearing poor Walter still nearer the vortex of ruin. Around and around upon the eddies of the deep black waters he was rushing, unmindful of all things only to satisfy the burning thirst that was consuming body and soul.

"Can he not be saved in some way?" Mr. Winters asked, half eagerly, of Henry Weston, one day.

"I am afraid not," was the sad reply.   He is very near the end of his race.   But others may be kept from sharing a similar fate if we all go to work for God and humanity.   It is high time, I think, to wake up and perform our duty.   Harry Allen will soon be drifting among the breakers, unless something be done to save him."

The minister of God started as these words came to his ears, and then he asked, "is Harry in danger — has he learned to drink ?"

" O yes," was the quick reply ; "you ought to have known that without asking. It could not well have been otherwise. Have you not noticed his unusual appearance of late ? His flushed face, and the unnatural brightness of his eyes, tell the sad story. Yet he confessed it all to me, only yesterday, but refused to go away from the tempter's power. The spell is upon him, yet he thinks that he can shake it off at any time."

" How did he get into this way. I thought that Mr. Freeland promised Mrs. Allen that her son should not meddle with the liquor ?"

and Mr. Winter's voice was husky with emotion.

"You cannot always depend upon the promise of one who sells liquor for his bread, even if he is a model landlord," Mr. Weston replied. " But then, I do not know just how Harry learned to drink, yet he thought that there was no danger in drinking wine and beer, as he confessed. I suppose that he has heard good men defend Mr. Freeland in his business."

A crimson flush came over Mr. Winter's face, and he only said :

" I wish that we could save him."

" Perhaps we can," was the answer. " I have been thinking of a new way in which I think a vast amount of good might be done. A society has been formed in a neighboring town, founded upon the principles of total abstinence. I do not know its name, but shall take pains to find out more about it. Its members cannot touch anything that contains alcohol — not even new cider. I am convinced that this is the right way to advocate temperance, and the only firm basis upon which to stand. All others are unsafe, and will crumble to the earth. But we must have your aid, Mr. Winters, and you must begin the work by preaching a good temperance sermon."

"A temperance sermon," Mr. Winters repeated; but then he suddenly stopped, for a span of horses was seen approaching at a terrible speed, and the carriage attached to them almost sailing through the air.

"It is Freeland's team, as I live!" said Mr. Weston, "and there are persons in the carriage—a boy—it is little Phil!"

Just at that moment the wheels of the carriage came in contact with a stone by the roadside, and the wagon bounded into the air, striking the ground with such force ·that the boy was pitched with great force into the road.

"What does it all mean?" Mr. Winters asked, as he glanced at Harry Allen, who was in the driver's place with the reins firmly grasped in one hand, whi ·he was applying the whip with the other, and urging the frightened horses at a still greater speed. "The boy is mad!" he continued, and then he rushed after Mr. Weston toward little Phil, who lay senseless in the dust.

"He is drunk, Mr. Winters, and I guess little Phil is dead," said Weston, as he lifted the body from the dust. "It will nearly kill Payne, for he fairly worships the boy."

This happened near the home of Mr. Weston, who lived just out of the village, and so little Phil was borne into his house. In a few moments a dozen men or more, pale and breathless, rushed along the road, in quest of the missing boy. Mr. Payne was among them, and soon stood moaning and weeping over his mangled son. The old physician was called, who carefully examined the boy.

"He is not dead," he said, as he detected a slight flutter about the heart. "But I don't believe that he can live, for he has been deeply injured, poor boy."

Slowly the almost crushed out life returned to the boy. First, there was nothing but the flutter of life-blood about the heart, and at intervals the pulse beat feebly. Then the breath came in a quick, spasmodic way ; and at last low, mournful groans were heard like sounds far in the distance. For many long hours the little life remaining in the mangled body,.would ebb almost away, and then return again. Several times the watchers thought that the last spark of life had gone out in darkness, but soon again some little gleam would reveal itself. Thus the suffering one lingered for days upon the borders of death-land—wandering to the very verge of the river. He suffered severely, moaning and crying nearly all of the time, while the agonized father bent tenderly over him. But, after a while, the pain seemed to partially leave him, and his hold upon life became a little stronger. Yet a strange, cruel truth became apparent, and that was that he would always be a poor, helpless cripple.

A few bitter words fell from the lips of Mr. Payne, who had not learned to bear the heavy burdens of life in a Christ-like way. Strange to say, when little Phil was able to be moved, he was conveyed to the home of Mr. Payne's sister, which was henceforth to be his abiding place. The father went also to watch over the helpless, deformed child. The second cruel lesson that this man received opened his long-blinded eyes.

CHAPTER XIV.

THE MASK THROWN OFF.

 SHORT time after Mr. Payne removed to his sister's house, a strange affair transpired in the hotel of Mr. Freeland. It was termed by the village paper, a " Stabbing Affray," and then followed a brief account of it all. The " affray " was enacted by two " gentlemen boarders," who had for some time been at Mr. Freeland's.

Nothing was known about the character of these two men, but as they dressed finely, and displayed occasionally well-filled wallets, they were regarded as gentlemen of the highest type, as they claimed to be. It was not known just how this " affray " began, but everybody knew how it ended. As the cry for "help," was heard, a couple of policemen soon came and arrested both parties, and placed them in the "lock up." A pack of cards were found scattered over the floor, and a pile of money upon the table, and then a few bottles of wine stood close by, which had been the active principle of the "affray." This happened up in one of the back chambers of the hotel, which was guarded by a strong lock and key. One of these "gentlemen," had received a slight wound which caused him to cry wildly out for "help." The other escaped uninjured, save a few rough knocks that the policemen gave him. The "affair" did not prove to be a very serious one, after all, save in one respect. That was, that it ruined the reputation of Mr. Freeland, and people no longer called him the "model landlord." It brought to light the fact, that gambling had been allowed and carried on upon quite a large scale. This was a very black stain upon the reputation of the man who had stood so high in the estimation of the people. And then the sad affair, when little Phil Payne was injured so severely, did not help the matter any. It was known by all that Harry Allen had drank nothing but the pure wine, that had been extolled so highly, when poor little Phil came so near being killed. People began to be very suspicious of Mr. Freeland, and watched closely for new developments. The most respectable portion of community began to shun him, but the low drinking class commenced at once to visit him, in his fine bar-room.

And how did the proud-spirited landlord bear up under this? Did he also become convinced of his great sin and repent ? No, HE only threw off his mask, and went on with his sad business. He had succeeded well under the disguise, and he undoubtedly would succeed equally as well without it, in a financial point of view. Of course, it was much more pleasant to carry on the traffic in good style, and have the approval of society at large, but if this could not be done, he must choose the other way.

It was a hard matter for him to haul down his false colors and work in his true character. He struggled hard against fate, but was obliged to yield at last. Circumstances beyond his control had conspired against him, and he could only curse his ill-luck, as he termed it all. It sounded very strangely to hear Mr. Andrew Freeland "swear," which he did very earnestly, after George Payne went away, declaring his intention to fight against intemperance. And when Mr. Winters preached the temperance sermon, and with tears streaming down his face, made a public confession of his error, the landlord's wrath knew no bounds, and he declared, in a loud angry voice, that he would be revenged in some way.

Then a strange, hateful look came over his face, and in less than an hour it was known throughout the village that all kinds of liquor would be sold by the " model landlord," and that all classes were invited to visit his hotel. Everybody was surprised at this, save Mr. Weston, who only said, "just as I expected."

" The time has fully come when we must strike a telling blow for temperance. Public sentiment has changed within the last six months, and our way is now open," Mr. Weston said to the now fully aroused minister of the gospel.

"Yes, we will go to work in right good earnest," Mr. Winters replied.

CHAPTER XV.

THE BLOW AND ITS RESULTS.

HE poor old mother of Walter Payson was dying. Some called her disease "old age," others a broken heart. It seemed rather strange that one so near the end of life's journey should die of a broken heart, yet it was true that grief had much to do with the old woman's death. She had borne bravely up under the burdens of other years, but then hope shone upon her pathway and she loved and clung to her idols. But the toils of years had not weighed her down in the dust of bitterness, as had the one great grief of her life—Walter's downfall. After the husband's strong arm had forever gone, she seemed more deeply still to comprehend her sad position in the world. Like the shattered boat, after mast and compass were gone, she drifted out upon the shoals of despair.

"Walter, my son, come nearer," she feebly said, as her dim eyes caught a glimpse of the other land. "Come nearer, my son, to receive my parting blessing."

He—the erring son, went with a slow, halting step toward the low couch.

"Walter, my son, the angel of mercy stands by you to lead you back to the fold of the Good Shepherd, if you will only reach out your hand. Will you do this, my son?"

The wasted form of the "prodigal son" trembled slightly, and a half eager look came over the pale face. But it vanished in a moment, and he said, in a husky voice :

" No, mother, I am lost forever."

But the dying woman continued :

" The angel of mercy waits to lead you—the Father will meet you upon the way—the door is wide open. Go, my son—reach out your hand—trust, believe, and the appetite that is consuming you shall be taken away. Go, my son," she went on, speaking very earnestly, "and all will be well." Saying this, the old mother's life work was forever over, and the spirit went up to the angel land.

" Walter, we will help you," said Mr. Winters, who had witnessed the scene. " Promise me by the side of the white, calm face, that you will again seek to enter the fold."

Perhaps the good mother's spirit lingered by the erring one, before going up to the "white-robed company," or possibly there might have been scores of angels whispering in the young man's ears. There must have been, for he said, "I promise," and then he fell upon his knees, and wept like a child.

The old mother was laid-away in the valley's dust, and her son again sought to live the better life. The "grace of God was sufficient for him," for he conquered. A temperance brotherhood had been formed in the village, sustained by such men as Henry Weston, George Payne, and Mr. Winters. Walter joined it and was saved.

"We must get Harry Allen into our ranks in some way," Mr. Weston said to his friend Payne.

"If we could only get him away from Freeland, we might succeed," was the answer.

" We can get him away, I think. But we must first convince him that he is beyond the reach of the landlord, who has threatened him some terrible punishment if he goes away. The boy, in some degree, has seemed to realize his true position since little Phil was injured so badly. But he dare not seek to go out of the lion's cage, for fear the beast will spring up and devour him. I shall watch for an opportunity to undeceive him."

" God help you," Mr. Payne replied.

A fine opportunity soon presented itself, which was improved by Mr. Weston. Howard Allen came home for a visit, and as he could not go into Mr. Freeland's hotel, Harry was obliged to return home for a few days. Mr. Weston made several visits to the little cottage during this time, and sought to lead poor Harry out of the lion's cage.

It was a long time before he could convince the boy just how matters stood, and when at last he succeeded, the poor deluded victim yielded gladly to be led by the hand of his true friend. It was the mission of the temperance brotherhood to "save the fallen, and to keep others from falling." This was just the help that the weak boy needed, and it saved him. He was accompanied by Mr. Weston, when he went to Andrew Freeland's for his clothes and a hundred dollars of back pay. The landlord refused to pay him, or even give up the boy's clothing. But a polite note from the village lawyer made him change his mind.

"I'll pay off Henry Weston and the rest of these temperance fools," he muttered to the man who carried the money to Harry Allen.

Perhaps he did pay them in the devil's own

way, but he was obliged to exhibit the "cloven foot" at every step.

The "model landlord" was never more known in the busy village, but Andrew Freeland still existed there, performing the vile work of Satan.

The mystic brotherhood of temperance grew to gigantic proportions. It became a power for good in subduing intemperance, and leading its votaries up to a better life. It led many into the fold, where the tempter dared not enter. It "plucked many a brand from the burning," and kept others from walking in the ways of ruin. After two years of labor it snatched the implements of death from the hands of Andrew Freeland, and he was obliged to seek another place in which to drag souls to ruin. It planted the germs of truth in many a soul, while it held error and delusion in check. Under the grand motto of " Faith, Hope and Charity," it still exists, upheld and sustained by God's own strong hand. Its leaders struck a sure death-blow to the enemy's heart when they built upon this rock of Total Abstinence, and the blessed results forever will remain.

PUBLICATIONS

OF THE

NATIONAL TEMPERANCE SOCIETY

AND

PUBLICATION HOUSE.

HON. WM. E. DODGE,   T T SHEFFIELD,   J· N STEARNS,
President.   Treasurer   Cor Sec. and Pub Agt.

THE NATIONAL TEMPERANCE SOCIETY, organized in 1866 for the purpose of supplying a sound and able temperance literature, have already stereotyped and published over four hundred and fifty publications of all sorts and sizes, from the one-page tract up to the bound volume of 500 pages. This list comprises books, tracts, and pamphlets, containing essays, stories, sermons, arguments, statistics, history, etc., upon every phase, of the question. Special attention has been given to the department for

SUNDAY-SCHOOL LIBRARIES.

Seventy-one volumes have already been issued, written by some of the best authors in the land These have been carefully examined and approved by the Publication Committee of the Society, representing the various religious denominations and temperance organizations of the country, which consists of the following members:

These volumes have been cordially commended by leading clergymen of all denominations, and by various National and State bodies all over the land. The following is the list, which can be procured through the regular Sunday-School trade, or by sending direct to the rooms of the Society.

At Lion's Mouth. 12mo, 410 pages By Miss Mary Dwinell Chellis. **$1 25**

Adopted. 18mo, 236 pp. By Mrs. E. J Richmond, - - **60**

Andrew Douglass. 18mo, 232 pages, - - - - - **75**

Aunt Dinah's Pledge. 12mo, 318 pages. By Miss Mary Dwinell Chellis, - - - - **1 25**

Alice Grant; or, Faith and Temperance. 12mo, 352 pages. By Mts. E. J. Richmond, - - - **1 25**

All for Money. 12mo, 340 pages. By Miss Mary Dwinell Chellis. **$1 25**

Barford Mills. 12mo, 246 pages. By Miss M. E. Winslow, **1 00**

Best Fellow in the World, The. 12mo, 352 pages. By Mrs. J. McNair Wright, - - - **1 25**

Broken Rock, The. 18mo, 139 pages. By Kruna, - - - **50**

Brook, and the Tide Turning, The. 12mo, 220 pages, - **1 00**

ome Home, Mother. 18mo, 143 pp. By Nelsie Brook. Illustrated with six choice engravings, - **$0 50**

rinking Fountain Stories, The. 12mo, 192 pages, - - **1 00**

umb Traitor, The. 12mo, 336 pp. By Margaret E. Wilmer, **1 25**

va's Engagement Ring. 12mo, 189 pp. By Margaret E. Wilmer, **90**

cho Bank. 18mo, 269 pages. By Evie, - - - - **85**

sther Maxwell's Mistake. 18mo, 236 pp. By Mrs. E N. Janvier **1 00**

anny Percy's Knight-Errant. 12mo, 267 pp. By Mary Graham, **1 00**

atal Dower, The. 18mo, 220 pp. By Mrs. E. J. Richmond, **60**

ire Fighters, The. 12mo, 294 pp. By Mrs. J. E. McConaughy, **1 25**

red's Hard Fight. 12mo, 334 pp. By Miss Marion Howard, **1 25**

rank Spencer's Rule of Life. 18mo, 180 pp. By John W. Kirton, - - - : - **50**

rank Oldfield; or, Lost and Found. 12mo, 408 pp , - **1 50**

ertie's Sacrifice; or, Glimpses at Two Lives. 18mo, 189 pp. By Mrs. F. D. Gage, - - - **50**

lass Cable, The. 12mo, 288 pp. By Margaret E Wilmer, - **1 25**

ard Master, The. 18mo, 278 pp. By Mrs. J. E. McConaughy, **85**

arker Family, The. 12mo, 36 pp. By Emily Thompson, - **1 25**

istory of a Threepenny Bit. 18mo, 216 pp., - - - **75**

istory of Two Lives, The. By Mrs. Lucy E. Sandford 18mo, 132 pp. A tale of actual fact, with an intro-

Hopedale Tavern, and What it Wrought. 12mo, 252 pp By J. Wm. Van Namee, - - - **$1 00**

Hole in the Bag, and Other Stories, The By Mrs. J. P. Ballard. 12mo, - - - - - **1 00**

How Could he Escape? 12mo, 324 pp By Mrs. J. McNair Wright, - - - - - **1 25**

Humpy Dumpy. 12mo, 316 pp. By Rev. J. J. Dana, - **1 25**

Jewelled Serpent, The. 12mo, 271 pp. By Mrs E. J. Richmond, **1 00**

John Bentley's Mistake. 18mo, 177 pp. By Mrs. M. A. Holt, **50**

Job Tufton's Rest. 12mo, 332 pp., - - - - **1 25**

Jug-or-Not. 12mo, 346 pp. By Mrs. J. McNair Wright, - **1 25**

Life Cruise of Captain Bess Adams, The. 12mo, 413 pp. By Mrs. J. McNair Wright, - - - **1 50**

Little Girl in Black. 12mo, 212 pp. By Margaret E. Wilmer, **90**

McAllisters, The. 18mo, 211 pp. By Mrs. E. J. Richmond, - **50**

Model Landlord, The. 18mo, 202 pp. By Mrs. M. A. Holt, - **60**

More Excellent Way, A, and Other Stories By M. E. Winslow. 12mo, 217 pages, - - - **1 00**

Mr. Mackenzie's Answer. 12mo, 352 pp. By Faye Huntington, **1 25**

National Temperance Orator, The. 12mo, 288 pp. By Miss L. Penney, - - - : **1 00**

Nettie Loring. 12mo, 352 pp. By Mrs. Geo. S. Downs, - **1 25**

Norman Brill's Life Work. By Abby Eldridge. 12mo, 218 pp., **1 00**

Nothing to Drink. 12mo, 400

The National Temperance Society's Books.

Old Brown Pitcher, The. 12mo, 222 pp. By the author of "Susie's Six Birthdays," - - - - **$1 00**

Old Times. 12mo, 351 pp. By Miss M. D. Chellis, - - **1 25**

Out of the Fire. 12mo, 420 pp. By Miss Mary Dwinell Chellis, **1 25**

Our Parish. 18mo, 252 pp. By Mrs. Emily Pearson, - - **75**

Packington Parish, and the Diver's Daughter. 12mo, 327 pp. By M. A. Paull, - - - - **1 25**

Paul Brewster & Son. By Helen A Chapman. 12mo, 238 pp., **1 00**

Philip Eckert's Struggles and Triumphs. 18mo, 216 pp. By the author of "Margaret Clair," - **60**

Pitcher of Cool Water, The. 18mo, 180 pp. By T. S. Arthur. **50**

Rachel Noble's Experi- ence. 18mo, 325 pp. By Bruce Edwards, - - - - - **90**

Red Bridge, The. 18mo, 321 pp. By Thrace Talman, - - **90**

Roy's Search; or, Lost in the Cars 12mo, 364 pp By Helen C Pearson, - - - - **1 25**

Rev. Dr. Willoughby and his Wine 12mo, 458 pp By Mrs Mary Spring Walker, - - **1 50**

Seymours, The. 12mo, 231 pp By Miss L Bates, - - **1 00**

Silver Castle. By Margaret E. Wilmer 12mo, 340 pages, - **1 25**

Temperance Doctor, The. 12mo, 370 pp By Miss Mary Dwinel Chellis, - - - - - **1 25**

Temperance Speaker, The. By J N Stearns, - - - - **75**

Temperance Anecdotes. 12mo, 288 pp, - - - - **1 00**

Tom Blinn's Temperance Society, and Other Stories 12mo, 316 pp **1 25**

Time Will Tell. 12mo, 307 pp By Mrs Wilson, - - **1 0**

Tim's Troubles. 12mo, 35 pp By M A. Paull, - - **1 5**

Vow at the Bars. 18mo, 1 pp, - - - - - - **40**

Wealth and Wine. 12mo 320 pp By Miss Mary Dwinell Chellis **1 25**

White Rose, The. By Mary J Hedges 12mo, 320 pp, - **1 25**

Work and Reward. 18mo 183 pp By Mrs M A Holt, - **5**

Zoa Rodman. 12mo, 262 pp By Mrs E J Richmond, - **1 0**

MISCELLANEOUS PUBLICATIONS.

Alcohol: Its Place and Power By James Miller and The Use and Abuse of Tobacco By John Lizars, **$1 00**

Alcohol: Its Nature and Effects By Charles A. Story, M D., **90**

Bacchus Dethroned. 12mo, 248 pp. By Frederick Powell, **1 00**

Band of Hope Manual. Per dozen, - - - - - **60**

Bases of the Temperance Reform, The. 12mo, 224 pp. By Rev Dawson Burns, - - - **1 00**

Bound Volume of Tracts. No 1. 500 pp, - - - **1 00**

Bound Volume of Tracts. No. 2. 384 pp, - - - **1 00**

Bound Volume of Sermons, **1 50**

Bible Rule of Temperance, By Rev. Geo. Duffield, D.D., - **60**

Bible Wines; or, The Laws of Fermentation and Wines of the Ancients 12mo, 139 pp By Rev Wm Patton, D D. Paper, **30** cts., cloth, **60**

Bound Volume of Almanac for 1869, '70, '71, '72, '73, '74, '75, '76, **1 00**

Centennial Temperance Memorial Volume. This is a large octavo volume of 1,000 pages, containing the full report of the proceedings of the International Temperance Conference in Philadelphia in June, 1876, and a history of the different temperance organizations in this country and Europe, also valuable essays on almost every phase of the question. Sold by subscription **5 00**

Catechism on Alcohol. Per dozen, - - - - - **60**

Communion Wine; or, Bi- ble Temperance By Rev Wm Thayer Paper, **20** cts, cloth, - - **50**

Cup of Death, The. A Concert Exercise 16 pages By Rev W F Crafts 6 cts each, per doz., **$0 60**

Delavan's Consideration of the Temperance Argument and History, **1 50**

Drops of Water. 12mo, 133 pp By Miss Ella Wheeler, - **75**

Four Pillars of Tempe- rance By J W Kirton, - - **75**

Forty Years' Fight with the Drink Demon. 12mo, 400 pp. By Chas Jewett, M.D., - - **1 50**

Hints and Helps for Woman's Christian Temperance Work By Miss Frances E Willard 12mo, 72 pp., **25**

Liquor Laws of the United States, - - - - - **25**

Lunarius: A Visitor from the Moon, - - - - **35**

Medical Use of Alcohol, The. By James Edmunds, M D Paper, **25** cts ; cloth, - - - **60**

National Temperance Al- manac, - - - - **10**

On Alcohol. By Benjamin W. Richardson, M A, F R S, of London, with an introduction by Dr Willard Parker, of New York 12mo, 190 pp Paper covers, **50** cts , cloth, **1 00**

Our Wasted Resources; or, The Missing Link in the Temperance Reform. By Wm. Hargreaves 12mo, 220 pp, - - - - **1 25**

Packet of Assorted Tracts, No. 1 Comprising Nos 1 to 53 of our list, making 250 pp, - - - **25**

Packet of Assorted Tracts, No. 2 Comprising Nos 53 to 100, making 250 pp., - - - - **25**

Packet of Assorted Tracts, No 3 Comprising Nos. 100 to 150 of our list, making 240 pages, - - **25**

Packet of Temperance Leaflets, No. 1. 128 pp, - - **10**

The National Temperance Society's Books.

Packet of Temperance Leaflets, No. 2. By T S. Arthur 128 pp, - - - - - **$0 10**

Packet of Prohibition Documents, - - - - **25**

Packet of Crusade Documents, - - - - **25**

Packet No. 1 of Pictorial Tracts for Children, - - - **25**

Packet No. 2 of Pictorial Tracts for Children, - - - **25**

Prohibition Does Prohibit; or, Prohibition not a Failure. 12mo, 48 pp. By J. N. Stearns, - - **10**

Scripture Testimony against Intoxicating Wine. By Rev. Wm. Ritchie, - - - - - **60**

Temperance Cyclopædia. By Rev. J B. Wakeley. 12mo, 244 pp.. **2 00**

Temperance Lesson Leaves No. 1, 2, 3. each 8 pp By Rev D. C Babcock Per 100, - - **$1 00**

Temperance Catechism Per dozen, - - - - **6**

Temperance Exercise. B Rev. Edmund Clark, - - - **1**

Text-Book of Temperance By Dr. F. R Lees, - - - **1 5**

Two Ways, The. A Conce Exercise 16 pp. By George Thayer. cts each; per dozen, - - - **6**

Woman's Temperance Crusade, The. By Rev. W. C. Steele, with an introduction by Dr. Dio Lewis. 12mo 83 pp., - - - - - **25**

Zoological Temperance Convention By Rev. Edward Hitchcock, D D., - - - - - **75**

PAMPHLETS.

Bound and How; or, Alcohol as a Narcotic By Charles Jewett, M D. 12mo, 24 pp, - - **10**

Buy Your Own Cherries. By John W Kirton 12mo, 32 pp, **20**

Example and Effort. By Hon S Colfax 12mo, 24 pp, - **15**

Father Mathew. Address by Hon Henry Wilson. 12mo, 24 pp, **15**

Illustrated Temperance Alphabet, - - - - - **25**

John Swig. A Poem. By Edward Carswell. 12mo, 24 pp Illustrated with eight characteristic engravings, printed on tinted paper, - **15**

On Alcohol. By Benjamin W. Richardson, M.A., M D., F.R S., of London, with an introduction by Dr. Willard Parker, of New York. 12mo 190 pages. Cloth, $1, paper covers, **50**

Prohibition Does Prohibit; or, Proh.bit on Not a Failure. By J. N Stearns. 12mo, 48 pp., - - **10**

Proceedings of National Temperance Conventions held in Saratoga in 1865, Cleveland in 1868, Saratoga in 1873, Chicago in 1875; each, - **25**

Rum Fiend, The, and Other Poems. By William H. Burleigh 12mo, 46 pp. Illustrated with three wood engravings, designed by Edward Carswell, - - - - - **20**

Scriptural Claims of Total Abstinence. By Rev. Newman Hall 12mo, 6½ pp., - - - - **15**

Suppression of the Liquor Traffic. A Prize Essay, by Rev. H D. Kitchell, President of the Middlebury College 12mo, 48 pp., - - **10**

Temperance and Education. 18mo, 34 pp By Mark Hopkins, D.D., President of Williams College, **10**

MUSIC AND SONG BOOKS.

Band of Hope Melodies.
Paper, - - - - - **$0 10**

Bugle Notes for the Tempe-
rance Army. Edited by W. F. Sherwin
and J N. Stearns. Price, paper, **30**
cts ; boards, - - - - **35**
Board covers, per doz , - - **4 00**
Paper covers, per doz., - - **3 40**

Campaign Temperance
Hymns, for Temperance Singers every-
where. 30 hymns, 24 pp Per 100, **3 00**

Our Songs. 8 pages. Containing 17 hymns suitable for public meetings. Per 100, - - - - **1 00**

Ripples of Song. Price **15** cts.,
paper covers; per 100, **$12.** Board
covers, **20** c s ; per 100, - **$18 00**

Temperance Hymns in sheet
form, size 9½ x 7½ inches, containing
hymns suitable for Public Temperance
Gatherings and Organizations. Price,
on thick paper, **$2** per hundred ; on card
board, **$5** per hundred.

Temperance Chimes. Price,
in paper, **30** cts. ; board covers, **35**
Board covers, per doz., - - **4 00**
Paper covers, per doz , - - **3 40**

Temperance Hymn-Book.
Price, paper covers, **12** cts. each ; **$10**
per 100 Board covers, **15** cts each,
per 100, - - - - - **13 00**

TWENTY-FOUR PAGE PAMPHLETS.

Five Cents each ; Sixty Cents per Dozen.

Is Alcohol Food ? By Dr. F.
R. Lees

Adulteration of Liquors.
By Rev. J B Dunn.

A High Fence of Fifteen
Bars. By the author of "Lunarius."

Bible Teetotalism. By Rev.
Peter Stryker

Dramshops, Industry, and
Taxes. By A. Burwell.

Drinking Usages of Society.
By Bishop Alonzo Potter.

Duty of the Church toward
the Present Temperance Movement,
The. By Rev. Isaac J Lansing.

Fruits of the Liquor Traf-
fic By Sumner Stebbins, M.D

Gentle Woman Roused. By
Rev. E P. Roe.

History and Mystery of a
Glass of Ale. By J. W Kirton.

Is Alcohol a Necessary of
Life? By Prof. Henry Munroe.

Liquor Traffic, The—The
Fallacies of its Defenders. By Rev E
G. Read.

Medicinal Drinking. By
Rev. John Kirk.

Physiological Action of
Alcohol. By Prof. Henry Munroe.

Son of My Friend, The. By
T. S. Arthur.

Stimulants for Women. By
Dr. James Edmunds, M.D.

Throne of Iniquity, The.
By Rev. A. Barnes.

Will the Coming Man Drink
Wine? By James Parton, Esq

Woman's Crusade, The—A
Novel Temperance Movement. By Dr.
D H. Mann.

TEMPERANCE SERMONS.

Fifteen Cents Each.

The National Temperance Society have published a series of Sermons in pamphl
form upon various phases of the temperance question, by some of the leading clerg
men in America. Bound in one volume in cloth, $1 50.

1. **Common Sense for Young** Men. By Rev. Henry Ward Beecher.

2. **Moral Duty of Total Ab-**stinence. By Rev. T L. Cuyler

3. **The Evil Beast.** By Rev. T. De Witt Talmage.

4. **The Good Samaritan.** By Rev. J. B. Dunn.

5. **Self-Denial: a Duty and** a Pleasure. By Rev J P. Newman, D D.

6. **The Church and Tempe-**rance. By John W. Mears, D D, Professor of Hamilton College, New York.

7. **Active Pity of a Queen.** By Rev John Hall, D.D.

8. **Temperance and the** Pulpit By Rev. C. D. Foss, D.D.

9. **The Evil of Intempe-**rance. By Rev. J. Romeyn Berry.

10. **Liberty and Love.** B Rev. Henry Ward Beecher.

11. **The Wine and th** Word. By Rev. Herrick Johnso

12. **Strange Children.** B Rev. Peter Stryker.

13. **The Impeachment an** Punishment of Alcohol. By Re C. H. Fowler

14. **Drinking for Health.** B Rev. H C. Fish.

15. **Scientific Certaintie** (not Opinions) about Alcohol B Rev. H. W. Warren.

16. **My Name is Legion.** B Rev. Stephen H. Tyng, D.D

17. **The Christian Servin** his Generation By Rev. Wm. M Taylor, A.M.

TEMPERANCE TRACTS.

The National Temperance Society publish a series of tracts, among which are 1
12mo tracts, from one to twelve pages each, 72 18mo Illustrated Children's Tract
all of which are put up in neat packets. Price 25 cents each.

Sixteen Temperance Leaflets, envelope size, in packets, 10 cents each.

LITHOGRAPHS AND POSTERS.

The Second Declaration of Independence Size 12 x 19 inches Per 100, - - - - - - **3 00**

Five Steps in Drinking, 15

An Honest Rumseller' Advertisement Per 100, - **1 0**

The Total Abstainer' Daily Witness and Bible Verdict, **7**

BAND OF HOPE SUPPLIES.

Band of Hope Manual. Per dozen, - - - **$0 60**

Temperance Catechism. Per dozen, - - - - **60**

Band of Hope Melodies. Paper, - - - - - **10**

Band of Hope Badge. Enamelled, $1 25 per dozen; 12 cts. singly. Plam. $1 per dozen; 10 cts. singly. Silver and Enamelled, each, - - **50**

National Temperance Orator, - - - - - **1 00**

Ripples of Song. Paper covers, 15 cts.; per 100, $12 Board covers, 20 cts., per 100, - - **18 00**

Juvenile Temperance Speaker, - - - - **25**

Illuminated Pledge Card. Per hundred, - - - **2 00**

Temperance Medal. 10 cts. each; per dozen - - - **$1 00**

Temperance Exercise. **10**

Illuminated Temperance Cards Set of ten, - - - **35**

Juvenile Temperance Pledges Per hundred, - - **3 00**

Certificates of Membership. Per hundred, - - - - **3 00**

Band of Hope Certificate and Pledge Combined (in colors). Per hundred, - - - - **4 00**

Temperance Lesson Leaves Nos 1, 2, 3, each 8 pp Per 100, - - - - - **1 00**

The Temperance Speaker. **75**

Catechism on Alcohol. By Miss Julia Colman. Per dcz., **60**

TEMPERANCE PLEDGES.

1. Sunday - school Pledge, 20x28 inches, in colors, each, **$0 25**

2. National Pledge, 20 x 28 inches, in colors, each, - **25**

3. Family Pledge, 20 x 14 inches, each, - - - **30**

4. Family Pledge, 13½ x 10½ inches, per 100, - - **2 00**

5. National Pledges, for circulation at public meetings, per 100, **50**

6. Children's Illustrated Pledge, 9½ x 6 inches, per 100, **3 00**

7. Children's Illustrated Pledge, not including tobacco, and Certificate combined, 12 x 9½ inches, in colors, per 100, **4 00**

8. Children's Illustrated Certificate of Membership, 9½ x 6 inches, per 100, - - **3 00**

9. Children's Band of Hope Pledge, which includes tobacco and profanity, and Certificate combined, 12 x 9½ inches, in colors, per 100, - - - - **$4 00**

10. Pocket Pledge-Book, with space for 80 names, - **10**

11. Sunday-school Pledge- Book, space for 1,000 names, **1 50**

12. National Temperance Pledge-Book, space for 1,000 names, - - - - **1 50**

13. Temperance Pledge- Card, 3½ x 5 inches, in colors, per 100, - - - - - **1 00**

14. Illuminated Pledge- Card, per 100, - - **2 00**

Druggists', Property-Holders', Grocers', Dealers', Physicians', and Citizens' Pledges, per 100, - - **75**

The National Temperance Society's Books.

TEMPERANCE DIALOGUES.

Trial and Condemnation of Judas Woemaker 15 cents. Per dozen, - - - - - **$1 50**

The First Glass; or, The Power of Woman's Influence; and

The Young Teetotaler; or, Saved at Last. 15 cents for both. Per dozen, - - - - - **1 50**

Reclaimed; or, The Danger of Moderate Drinking 10 cents. Per dozen, - - - - - **1 00**

Marry No Man if He Drinks. 10 cents. Per dozen, **1 00**

Which Will You Choose 36 pages. By Miss M. D. Chellis 1 cents. Per dozen, - - - **$1 5**

Wine as a Medicine. 1 cents. Per dozen, - - - **1 0**

The Stumbling Block. 1 cents. Per dozen, - - - **1 0**

Aunt Dinah's Pledge. Dra matized from the Book, - - 1

The Temperance Doctor Dramatized from the Book, - 1

Shall I Marry a Moderat Drinker? 10 cents. Per dozen, **1 0**

THE YOUTH'S TEMPERANCE BANNER.

The National Temperance Society and Publication House publish a beautifully-illu' trated four-page monthly paper for children and youths, Sabbath-schools, and juvenil temperance organizations. Each number contains several choice engravings, a piece c music, and a great variety of articles from the pens of the best writers for children i America

Its object is to make the temperance work and education a part of the religious cu ture and training of the Sabbath-school and family circle, that the children may be earl taught to shun the intoxicating cup, and walk in the path of truth, soberness, an righteousness.

The following are some of the writers for THE BANNER Mrs. J. P. Ballard (Kruna Miss M. D. Chellis, Mrs. Nellie H Bradley, Rev. Wm M Thayer, Edward Carswel Geo W. Bungay, J. H. Kellogg, Mrs. J. E. McConaughy, Mrs. M. A. Dennison, Mr E. J. Richmond, Rev. S. B. S. Bissell, Rev. Alfred Taylor, Mrs. M. A. Kidder, etc etc.

THE BANNER has already been welcomed into thousands of Sabbath-schools of all d nominations as the only youth's temperance paper published for Sabbath-schools.

Terms, cash in advance, including postage.

Single copy, one year,	-	-	**$0 35**	Thirty copies, to one address,	**$4 0**		
Eight copies, to one address,	-		**1 08**	Forty " " "	-	**5 4**	
Ten " " "			**1 35**	Fift " " "	-	**6 7**	
Fifteen " " "		-	**2 03**	Oney hundred copies, to one			
Twenty " " "		-	**2 70**	address,	-	- -	**13 0**

We trust the friends of temperance and Sunday-schools will make the effort to intr duce THE BANNER into every Sunday-school in their midst, as the price at which it published—which does not cover the cost of paper and printing—prevents the seudu of agents to introduce it

The National Temperance Society's Books.

THE NATIONAL TEMPERANCE ADVOCATE.

The National Temperance Society and Publication House publish a monthly paper devoted to the interests of the temperance reform, which contains articles upon every phase of the movement from the pens of some of the ablest writers in America, among whom are· Rev. T. L. Cuyler, D.D , Dr. Charles Jewett, Rev. Wm Goodell, A. M· Powell, Rev Peter Stryker, Rev. J B Dunn, Rev. Wm M. Thayer, Rev Wm. Patton, D D., Geo. W. Bungay, Mrs. F M Bradley, Miss M. D Chellis, Kruna, etc., etc.

It also contains a history of the progress of the movement from month to month in all of the States, which is of great value to every worker in the cause and to those who are in any way interested in the work, and no pains will be spared to make this full of the most valuable information to all classes in the community

Terms (cash in advance), including postage : One dollar and ten cents per year for single copies, ten copies to one address, $10; twenty copies to one address, $18; all over twenty copies at 90 cents per copy.

SEWALL'S STOMACH PLATES·

The National Temperance Society and Publication House have republished the celebrated lithographic drawings of the human stomach, showing the effects of intoxicating liquors, from the first inception of disease occasioned thereby, to death by delirium tremens. We have had repeated applications for them during the past few years, and have now reproduced them in the original form. The drawings are eight in number. Size, 27 x 34 inches

These drawings are not the production of mere fancy, but are the result of actual scientific research and investigation, in one living case (that of Alexis St. Martin, in the year 1822), and of others immediately after death They are invaluable to every student, scientific and medical man, and especially to those who are lecturing upon physiology or temperance. They should be in the possession of every college, school, temperance society, and reading-room in the land Price, $12 per set, plain paper; $15, mounted and on rollers.

All orders should be addressed to

J. N. STEARNS, Publishing Agent,

58 Reade Street, New York.

CPSIA information can be obtained
at www.ICGtesting.com
Printed in the USA
BVHW091354020119
536867BV00019B/365/P